SHORT HISTORIES CIRCLING CROWS

Imrah Baines

 New Generation Publishing

Contents

Phnom Penh, Cambodia.
April 1975

I

"…and her voice is so high, when she laughs she's like one of those jungle animals howling for sex. She's as *thick* as *Vietnamese* soup. I know Vietnamese soup isn't thick, it's just a metaphor. But anyway, it's just *her*, *all* of her. Do you understand? She's *so snobbish*, so *better* than everyone else, just because she has *two* jobs. She works *so hard* and has *no time* for anyone else because she's *so busy* and *important*. And she *never* misses an opportunity to mention she used to work for one of Norodum Sihanouk's ministries. And her husband works for a *foreign* company, a *European* company. How *glamorous*! She makes my blood boil sometimes. Do you understand? Do you? Hey, are you even listening to me?"

Phaly Nuon struck her wistful husband on the arm causing him to swerve and almost hit an oncoming motorcycle taxi.

"What are you doing? Do you want me to crash?"

"I asked you: Do you understand why Chit Lo makes my blood boil? Huh?"

Long Boret sighed and dutifully nodded.

"And the way she holds those *American* dollars in her hand, so everyone can see what a *rich bitch* she is; never mind them bombing our country. You know, she's *so proud* of being able to speak *French* and she's always talking about her student days in *Paris*… I *hate* her. She'd be happy if the French were still here, she'd be one of their lackeys. I wish she would go and live in *France*, I mean she's always going on about it. I'll tell you something else as well…"

Long Borat could hear the noise emanating from his wife's mouth but wasn't listening to it. Instead his mind couldn't get away from the numerous chores he had yet to do at work; there simply weren't enough hours in the day for the worn bread-winner, and with the civil war raging everything was twice as hard at the moment. The project his boss had assigned him to was more demanding than he had originally thought it would be; in short, he'd bitten off more than he could chew. But as is the way with Khmer culture, you don't admit something is too much for you once you've agreed to do it. To lose face with your boss was simply unacceptable – better to put a sword through one's stomach like those Japanese, thought Long Boret.

"Let's change Aki Ra's school," the husband thought aloud. "I don't like it."

Phaly Nuon, still ranting about Chit Lo, turned to her husband.

"What? Are you mad? Why? What's wrong with Chao Ponhea Yat? You know it's named after one of King Norodom Sihanouk's ancestors, not that that counts for anything these days. I can't believe he's in alliance with those Red Khmer; how about that? Royalists *and* Communists in bed together! And both of them bending over for the Vietnamese!"

"There's something I don't like about it. There always seem to be black crows circling above it. I just don't like it. I…"

"What black crows? You probably want to send her to one of those exclusive schools, like Chit Lo does with her spoilt brats. Well, what's wrong with state education? I won't have my socialist principles compromised for the sake of private education when my daughter can have just as good an education in a state school. Education should be free for everyone…"

Phaly Nuon would often defend socialist ideology to make out she was a socialist, though if truth be known she was no more a socialist than Ho Chi Minh was a democrat. Her badly-disguised deceit, however, was nothing more than a ruse to draw her mundanely passive husband into an argument, being that he was a staunch advocate of free trade principles.

Long Boret, though, had again stopped listening to his wife; in fact, he had stopped listening a long, long time ago. His ears were instead turned towards the gunfire and shells exploding in the distance. It was more soothing than his wife's voice, he thought.

Aki Ra came out of school with hundreds of other children all kicking up dust in the dry and humid heat. Those privileged enough to have parents with cars scrambled to find them. A few others jumped onto motorcycles or scooters and some jumped onto bicycles, where multiple family members would precariously balance. The overwhelming majority would walk home. Buses were too sporadic because of the war, and as for railways, they had yet to be built, it was only 1975 - Thursday April 17th 1975, to be precise.

"How's school?" The husband asked the son, completely ignoring his wife.

"Ok. Why did we get sent home early today, Dad? Mr Kol said the commie guerrillas have beaten the government."

"Really? What else did he say?"

"Only that if what happened in Kratie or Oudong is anything to go by, we're all in the shit."

"I don't think he used those exact words, did he?"

"No, Dad. Sorry. What happened in Kratie and Oudong?"

"I don't know, son. The refugees that came here said that they emptied the town and made the people go and work in the countryside. We haven't been able to do business there since it fell. No one really knows, except those that are there."

"What'll happen to Phnom Penh if it's really fallen?"

"I don't know, son; but it's not a good situation. If the Americans really have left it gives the Communists *carte blanche…*"

"Now you're speaking French, just like Chit Lo! Am I not good enough for you because I can only speak Khmer? Would you prefer a more cultured wife? Someone bi-lingual? Like Chit Lo, perhaps?"

"It's just an expre…"

"Just drive the car!" angrily interjected the mother, patting down her frizzy, though stylish, black mop. "Such a drama queen! Frightening him! You make mountains from molehills. Everything will be back to normal in a couple of weeks, you'll see. There'll be a counter coup and Lon Nol will come back; or the Americans will change their minds again and return – that's if they've even left. Maybe the Vietnamese, but let's hope not – bastards can't stop meddling in our affairs, I'd rather the Thais. You know, even King Norodom Sihanouk could make a comeback if the Chinese help him. I really don't like him, but his wife wears such lovely dresses and shoes. Have you seen the pair she wore to…?"

Amidst the backdrop of gunfire and exploding shells Long Boret drove wearily through unusually half-deserted streets of the capital. The smell of durian and exotic fruits mingled now with rancid gunpowder. Jeeps could be seen carrying battled-hardened soldiers and red flags were being hoisted. People were again on the move. Things were changing; half deserted shops, homes and offices all wore the scars of a brutal battle: scorched with fire; littered with bullet holes; windows blown out from where mortars had struck. It was eerie, like being in a ghost town that was still occupied. The atmosphere had turned, that much was definite.

"You know, she wears these really *stupid* trousers – they've got a name for them but I can't remember what they're called, flarey or something. She told me that they're fashionable in *The West*. She looks *so stupid*. I said to her, well, I thought to myself, that this isn't *Europe* or *America*, this isn't *Paris, London*, or *Milan* or *Madrid*, it's *Phnom Penh* for goodness' sake. What a *stupid cow*, head so far up her own back side she can't see how *ridiculous* she looks. Have you seen her wearing them? She was wearing them last week, cream coloured trousers – tight around the thighs and they come out at the bottom. Did you see? I thought they were…"

Long Borat switched the radio on, not just for the faint hope of some news, but also to drown out his wife's incessant chattering. As he futilely searched for the BBC World Service, she suddenly turned to him to capture his attention, and softened her tone as well as her countenance.

"Darling…" Long Boret recognized the gentle tone and rolled his eyes. "Darling, when can we go on holiday again? It's been such a long time since we've been anywhere; and Aki Ra would love to go abroad again, wouldn't you dear?"

The boy shifted excitedly in his seat. "Yeah, can we go to Kuala Lumpur to see Muhammad Ali fight?"

"Well, Papa? Can we?" asked the lady with fluttering eye lids and a manipulative smile.

Long Boret had little patience left. "Look, forget the holiday. I keep saying we should leave for good; start a life in a stable country where we don't have to worry so much. We could have gone to Bangkok, we could be there by now, safe and secure, and settled. Their shops are full of food, ours are full of blood."

"What are you talking about? Why would you want to leave Cambodia? This is *our* home, *our* country. Why would we give up everything we've worked so hard for?"

"We?"

"All we need is a short break somewhere. Somewhere like Singapore or, like Aki Ra says, Kuala Lumpur. Imagine seeing Muhammad Ali fighting, wow, wouldn't that be amazing? Darling?"

"Holidays aren't free. How the hell are we going to afford one? We could maybe go to Sihanoukville for a weekend…"

"Sihanoukville? What? It'd be nice to leave the country at least."

"Well, if you'd like to get a job and save up to take us all on holiday, I'll support you a hundred per cent."

"It's not fair!" snapped Phaly Nuon. "Chit Lo's husband took her to Tokyo last year, and this year they're going to Hong Kong. Why can't you take me places? It's not fair. He's always buying her things. Why can't you buy *me* nice things? Why can't *I* go places? It's not fair. Chit Lo gets *everything*."

She crossed her arms and turned her back to her beleaguered husband. He was grateful for that, for her sulks; it gave him peace and quiet, leaving him with only the sounds of war for company.

II

No sooner had the Khmer Rouge come to power than they began to evacuate the capital.

"The Americans are going to bomb Phnom Penh, you must leave. *Now*!"

Phaly Nuon took exception to the soldier. At the best of times she never liked taking orders, least of all by a teenager young enough to be her son.

"To hell with the Americans! This is our home and we will stay here."

"You can't. You must leave. It's an order."

The soldier gave the lady a hard, cold stare. There was something in his eyes that told Phaly Nuon not to remonstrate. His face was emaciated; his uniform ripped and ragged, bags under his eyes and scars on his face. His countenance reflected that of a hardened warrior who had spent years brutally fighting his depraved enemy.

He tapped the butt of his rifle impatiently as Long Boret came to see what was happening.

"We have to leave," his wife told him. "The Americans are going to bomb."

"*What*?" came the incredulous shriek. "Where are we supposed to go?"

The soldier shrugged his shoulders giving Long Boret the same deadly stare he had given Phaly Nuon. A chill went down his spine. And Long Boret, just as wife, recognized that this was no time to remonstrate.

The couple returned inside. They collected all of their money, approximately fifteen hundred American dollars, and whatever jewellery they could conceal on their persons, before setting off in their car with no idea where they were actually heading to.

They joined the entire populace of the capital in a wild sea of humanity making up a tide of misery. People walked, struggling to carry precious, life-long possessions. Phaly Nuon and Long Boret momentarily contemplated giving up their car to join those on foot such was the heavy volume of human traffic, but the car was way too precious to abandon, so instead they inched forward, bit by bit, just hoping the Americans wouldn't start their bombing campaign. The parched earth only just withstood the mass of humanity. With trees, plants and vegetation all fully dehydrated, cracks now appeared and widened; and with the travelling hordes of people forever increasing it seemed for a while that the cracks in the earth would split wide open and swallow the city whole. At least that's what Phaly Nuon thought, for she had never seen such a wave of chaos coupled with misery – a wave upon which she and her family now precariously balanced.

"I love your hair."

Phaly Nuon turned to see Chit Lo gormlessly smiling at her. "Chit Lo! What are you doing here?"

"Oh, isn't it such a pain? These bloody Americans! Do you like my shoes?"

Chit Lo pointed to her toe to give her rather subdued friend a good view.

"Oh, they're lovely."

"Oh, thank you. They're from Europe, you know, *Paris*."

"Oh, wonderful."

"Do you like my hair?" Chit Lo gently patted her mop. "It's based on Bridget Bardot's new style."

"Where's Lop Top?" asked Long Boret, impatiently, with a creased forehead and sweat running down his brow.

"He's at work. I'm going there now to meet him."

"Where will you go?"

"I don't know. Lop Top said we'll go to the border…"

"You're leaving the country? Where are you going?"

"I don't know. The airport is closed."

"Doesn't Lop Top want to stay here? I mean all this bullshit will hopefully be over in a couple of days."

"He says it's too dangerous now the Americans have left. He says the Khmer Rouge aren't to be trusted."

"Who?"

"The Khmer Rouge, that's what they're calling themselves."

"Who's the leader? Who's our new president?"

"I don't know. What does it matter? As long as I don't ruin these shoes – they're real leather you know – from Paris."

Long Boret turned his gaze once again towards the heaving mass of misery and the murder of crows circling above.

"Good luck, then," smiled Chit Lo, as she turned to fight her way through the crowd.

Phaly Nuon glanced up the street, witnessing a family being forced out of their home with brute force; another person had feinted and seemed to be having some kind of fit; while someone else she saw lay prostrate on the ground having been smashed with a butt of a rifle. A nausea that had been building now came to surface and Phaly Nuon vomited. For the first time for a long time the husband showed some genuine sympathy by stroking back his wife's hair. With tears streaking down her cheeks, she turned to wave at her friend, but Chit Lo had been swallowed up by the crowd; either that or the cracks in the parched earth really had split wide open.

Jallianwala Bagh, Amritsar, Punjab, India.
19th April 1919

I

The decrepit old legs of Chumar Sahota languidly carried him to his master's study. With crossed legs, there sat plump and middle-aged David Singh, cross legged, sitting upon a cushion which sat upon a stone, cold floor. To his side stood a puny young boy in dirty rags, who was indeed fairly soiled; he stood with legs akimbo waving a giant fan, fanning the master. The solitary fan attached to the ceiling had been rendered useless by yet another power cut. The room itself, though fairly significant in size, was rather barren.

"Sahota! Come in, sit down. Do you want a glass of water? It's so bloody hot today. Maybe some chai?"

All offers of refreshments were declined; the master's unusual hospitality was clearly a bad omen.

"Everything ok?" smiled David Singh with absolutely no interest or sincerity in the question.

The old man merely nodded, too worn to go into the details of his exhausting day which had begun at 4:30am, had lasted for over twelve hours and still had another six hours to go. Moreover, he had no intention of wasting whatever breath he had left on such chit-chat. He placed his skeletal frame upon the cold, stone floor and sat crossed legged opposite his master.

"Look, Sahota. I've known you a long time. I mean, you were one of my father's servants, so I think of you as family; like an uncle. You've served us so well; working so hard for my family; attending to all sorts; never complaining; never causing problems; just quietly going about your work. You must be looking forward to the day when you can just retire."

"No, Sir. I will go on working for as long as God allows me to, just like my father and his father before him, my granddad."

"But unlike your father and grandfather you have the good fortune of knowing me," mischievously smiled David Singh, waxing his moustache.

From beneath his robe he produced a bundle of money and placed it with much satisfaction in front of his servant.

"There you go; a hundred rupees. Probably more money than you've ever seen. It's yours; your *retirement* money."

Chumar's eyes bulged wide open, displaying their veins, as he gawped at the money in astonishment; he had never seen such a sum. "I don't want to retire, Sir. I enjoy my work."

David Singh laughed. "You are old, like a battered broom, worn from sweeping too many harsh surfaces. You cannot work like a young man any more, no matter what you think. Lifting heavy things and things like that, it takes you so long. If you were a mule, which in a way you are, you'd be put down. Take the money and be grateful."

Chumar sat in total shock. He had been born in this very house and expected to die in it too. His liberty he did not want. He was far too old for change, no matter what that change was.

"Sir, what would I do with that money?"

"You can buy your own land, perhaps build a house; get some animals. Or you can go to Delhi, or Bombay, or to the coast. Maybe travel across the desert."

"I'm old, Sir. I do not need adventure."

David Singh's patience wore thin. His greasy smile slipped off his face and was replaced by a much sterner expression.

"I am not *asking* you, Chumar Sahota, I am *telling* you. You have no choice in the matter. You are surplus to requirements and with the bad harvest it is a struggle to keep you. Most people would release you without anything, just kick you out onto the street to live with the monkeys and get eaten by the tigers; but as you were thought of so highly by my father, and because of your service to us, and the fact I am the kindest man in British India, I am giving you this money so you don't need to worry about anything ever again. Now take it; you are free to go." He turned to the small boy waving the fan for him. "Come on, you bloody monkey, faster!"

Unable to fathom the situation, Chumar's over-worked mind was set to crumble. He sat rubbing his temples and frowning at the money.

"I have no need for all this money, Sir. I am a simple man…"

"I know that…"

"My only concern is my daughter, Sir. Please wait until she is married then do with me what you will. I beg you, Sir."

David Singh's demeanour suddenly morphed as he shifted uncomfortably on his silken cushion.

"Ah, yes. Just one thing… Your daughter won't be leaving with you. I still have use for her."

For the first time the servant looked his master in the eye. His shock was palpable.

"No, Sir, please. You said you wouldn't touch her, Sir. You said out of respect you would leave her alone. You said…"

"I'm not going to touch her. I promise you I won't lay a finger on her – unlike your cousin, who I had a great time with. Don't worry. Now please take the money and gather your belongings."

"You can't separate my daughter from me, Sir. She's the only one I have; she's all I have. Please, Sir. If you…"

"Don't worry. She'll be absolutely fine," smiled David Singh. "Now, if you don't mind, get out."

Chumar attempted to stand but his stick-like legs were weak from the exhaustion of the day's work coupled with the shock of this news.

"Sir, I cannot leave without her."

"Very well," snapped David Singh. "Then you stay and she goes."

"What? Sir?"

Exasperated with the illiterate man, David Singh now resorted to the truth.

"I have a man for your daughter."

"To marry? Sir?"

"Well, not exactly. He already has a wife – but she is far away."

The realization of what was to become of his daughter cut the old man to the bone. She was indeed all he had, and any life apart from her would destroy him. He knew that one day that day would come, when she would leave to be with another family; but not now, not like this. Once malaria had taken his wife he made a solemn vow to her to do all he could to give their only child a better life than they had had; his entire life had been a dedication to this solitary aim.

"You always promised my father no harm would come to us, Sir."

"And what harm has come to you? You have a hundred Rupees and your daughter is to be a concubine to one of the richest and most powerful men in the whole world."

"There are many other girls, Sir."

"Indeed there are, Sahota, but none have the glaring breasts that your daughter carries around with her."

22

Falling to his knees and begging would have done nothing to help, but Chumar tried nonetheless. He clutched and kissed David's Singh's feet while remonstrating and received a couple of kicks for his troubles. With comedic effect, David Singh grabbed the large fan from the young boy and battered Chumar with it. In the end, Sahota, as ever, did what he always did, he accepted his fate.

"He is a foreigner, an Englishman, a businessman, a man of wealth and esteem; a great man. And you should be grateful that your daughter has ended up in such an important man's harem. Uneducated people never appreciate anything, probably because they cannot understand anything, probably because they're uneducated. Fan me harder, monkey boy! Or you'll get fed with the dogs!"

The boy indeed further increased his tempo and regulated his breathing to manage his stitch. David Singh sighed upon viewing the pathetic figure of his servant.

"He will come here tonight, to get her, so you can say goodbye to her now. You do not need to leave, but take this, the money."

"I have no need, Sir…"

"*Take it*; it's yours. It eases my conscience. I had a vision where Vishnu came to me, no, it was Rama, or was it Ganesh? No, it was Hanuman, I think. Anyway, I was told to do something nice for you, so the money is for you; take it so I can feel better. Now go on, get out."

Reluctantly the old man took the bundle and slowly got to his feet, wiping away his sweat mingled tears. David Singh waved him away while scowling at the fan-waving boy.

"Bloody lazy monkey! Didn't I say faster? Why are you sweating, you're not doing anything?"

Chumar Sahota eventually reached the door. "Thank you, Sir," his old voice croaked, unnoticed, as he stumbled away.

II

Brigadier-General Thomas Warren Clive Battle finally approached the Singh house, swaying merrily upon the baffled mare upon which he sat. The entourage he bought with him had a congenial air about it: fellow soldiers drank and sang heartily with their superior, while the sober Indian slave contingent did their best to join in. Upon hearing the racket David Singh went running through his large house clicking his fingers and bellowing at the servants. His chubby body pounded the floor as he excitedly reached the fore of his house to greet his most auspicious guest. There he found the young, dashing Major, sprawled on his backside.

"Blasted horse! Speaks no English you know! Or Hindi it would seem!"

David Singh's own English was still developing; he tried, though, as he did with all things English.

"Actually people are speaking Punjabi here…"

"I care not for the language you Zulus speak. I only care for the Crown, and my penis! Ah, yes, splendid! What's your name, little man? You must excuse me, but all your names sound so exasperatingly foreign."

"It's being David, Sir; David Singh. Aren't you remembering?"

"Splendid! David? You don't look much like a David. I mean that's a good Christian sounding name."

"No, Sir. I was changing my name, upon your recommendation. You were recommending David for me. You're not remembering?"

"Was I? Splendid!"

The middle-aged Brigadier-General, old before his time, finally got to his feet with the aid of his host; he dusted down his military uniform, patted down his bush-like moustache then wrapped his arm around David Singh. "Come on then, young man. What say you we down this liquor and then you can show me this beauty?"

"Sir, I am not drinking. I am being a Sikh."

"Well, if you're sick then more for me. Splendid! Hoorah!"

A party was indeed had by all. Villagers came to see what all the fuss was and joined in the celebrations; eunuchs turned up and performed plays; dancers came; musicians drowned out the crickets and mosquitoes; beggars arrived and all sorts. David Singh was delighted. He had brought a white man to the village and now his standing was set to rocket. Indeed, many had yet to see a white person, including Chumar Sahota, who stood hiding behind a pillar, peering at the Brigadier-General, completely baffled by his foreign, drunken ways, his strange hair and clothes, and the peculiar noise emanating from his mouth. Inevitably, the master called him over to meet the strange foreigner.

"Sahota, come here, come here. This is Brigadier-General Battle; he is going to look after your daughter." David Singh turned to the Brigadier-General, switching from Punjabi to English. "Major, Sir, this is being father of woman who I was telling you about."

The Brigadier-General struggled to stay on his feet such was his intoxication. "Translate this to him, my good Hindu man, tell him: I'm going to give his daughter a bloody good rogering tonight, and a bloody good rogering every other night as well! Yes, it shall be splendid! I'll take her around this sub-continent with me and I'll subject her to all sorts of lurid acts in all sorts of terrain! Hoorah!"

The Brigadier-General stumbled backwards laughing while David Singh translated.

"He said he will take good care of your daughter. He says that she will travel all over India."

"Tell him to spend the two hundred rupees carefully."

"He says to spend the hundred rupees carefully."

"To hell with it… Spend it! Waste it! Enjoy it! Mount it!"

"He says to just spend the money. Give some to me maybe, if you like."

Sahota was still frightened and even more confused now. The actions of the strange foreigner didn't seem to match with his words – or with the translation at least.

"Please ask him to look after my daughter, Sir."

David Singh nodded. "Sir, he is saying that you are being free to doing whatever you are wishing with his daughter."

"Splendid! Tell him that my penis has sole responsibility for her!" Brigadier-General Battle roared his drunken laugh.

"He says that he will look after your daughter as if she is one of his own."

"He has children?" asked a shocked Chumar.

"Here you go, my darkened friend," slurred the military man as he handed Chumar a half drunken bottle of whiskey. "Here you go, a present from the civilized world; to say thank you. Now what say you get this beauty out so I can take her back for some debauched action? Hoorah!"

Chumar's petrified teenage daughter, Minder, was put into a carriage which the Brigadier-General was expected to follow on his horse, but such was his drunken state he was unable to mount the mare (not from want of trying) so instead joined his new virgin whore in the carriage.

"Don't be scared, my dear..." mumbled the wrinkled creature before dropping off.

As weary villagers waved off the foreign entourage Chumar suddenly appeared at the door of the carriage. He eyed the snoring foreigner sprawled unceremoniously over the seat, and then took one final look at his offspring. Neither father nor daughter could do anything to stem the flow of tears.

The horses neighed restlessly as they prepared to gallop.

"Here," said Chumar, putting his hand up his daughter's sari.

"Father!"

"Take it!"

She placed her hand over his and felt something.

"It's a hundred rupees. Take it!"

The carriage gave a sudden jolt then was away. And once the dust had settled and the cheering crowds gone home, there would be alone a silhouette of a withered and exhausted old man, crouching in the moonlight with only a half drunk bottle of whiskey, dried tears and a broken heart for company.

III

Perched upon the hill station known as Shimla was Brigadier-General Thomas Warren Clive Battle's residence: lush and palatial. The grand Victorian design looked decisively surreal within its environs of dry earth, parched trees and numerous beggars. Here the weather was a relief from the awful heat on the Indian plains, so much so in fact that the British military had turned the picturesque village into their summer capital.

Tucked away in a corner of the residence was a large, ill-furnished room which was out of bounds to soldiers and administrators. Hidden in the corner was a timid, young lady whose good looks had seemingly got her there. Yet it was those same good looks that would get her out.

Fortunately for Minder, no sooner had she arrived at her new abode than her new master had to leave. The Brigadier-General never had an opportunity to ravish his new beauty as once he had sobered up the following morning he was called away to Amritsar. There he remained for some time; he discovered that the natives had had the audacity to protest against British rule and such was the turmoil that he remained there for some time.

Charming looks coupled with money allowed Minder to escape the hills of Shimla and return to the plains. She bribed the guards five rupees each to allow her to escape from the rear; she gave five rupees to a boy who helped guide her through unfamiliar terrain; a farmer gave her a ride on his oxen for five rupees; a store keeper allowed her to hide from soldiers in his shop for another five; she paid ten rupees to a rickshaw wala who helped transport her back to her village, and the rest went on food.

Eight days after she had left and with funds vanquished, she arrived back in her village around midnight. The only noises that could be heard were those of the crickets and buzzing mosquitoes; otherwise an eerie stillness could be felt; a stillness that blanketed the entire village and extended to the former master's house. The house was a quarter wood and three-quarters brick (the wood for the servants and the brick for the master and his family).

Minder cautiously entered the squalid servant's quarters, tiptoeing straight to her room which she had shared with her father.

"Papa," she gently called, but not only was there no sign of her father, there was also no sign of anyone else. It was as if all life had become extinct, save for those crickets and mosquitoes.

She made her way into the main part of the house, the only indication of life being the repetitive drone of a newly installed ceiling fan. She followed the sound into the main living area: a large, square room which had been stripped of its furniture, only a few damaged wicker chairs remained. There was no-one there, or so she thought; though had she looked a little closer she would have found David Singh lurking in the corner.

"Papa," again she cried, like the howl of a lost baby fox calling for its mother.

She scoured the room for something, anything, cumbersomely feeling her way around in the dark.

"Minder?"

"Who's that?"

David Singh, finally brave enough to reveal himself, stepped out from behind the chair that he had been hiding behind; instantly the young lady recognized his chubby frame.

"What's happening? Where is everyone? Where's my father?"

"There is no-one here. Everyone has left."

"What? Why? My father?"

"He's gone too."

David Singh cautiously edged towards the young lady while explaining all.

"There was a massacre in Amritsar, maybe you know about it, maybe you do not. But they killed many people, and now many more people are angry. Some bloody Indians came running through the village looking for some Englishmen, or anyone who had anything to do with the English. Of course, they could not find any English because they are all up in Shimla. So these bloody yobs came here, threatening to kill me, to burn my house down. They ransacked the house, smashed the doors and the shutters, they looted my belongings, taking everything: furniture, bowls, spoons, clothes. They released all my cattle; they are wandering around somewhere, lost." He shook his head sadly at the thought.

"My father?"

"I don't know, he went with the yobs. All the servants have gone. I don't know where he is. Even my most loyal servant has deserted me."

Completely confounded and disheartened, Minder dropped her head, looking sadly at the cold, stone tiles. Without her father she was as disorientated as David Singh's cattle; without him she knew not what to do. Her heart splintered then sank. David Singh edged closer.

"Shouldn't you be with Mr Battle, the English military man? He paid a lot of money for you."

Minder avoided any eye contact and nervously began fingering her plat.

"No… He let me go…"

"He let you go?"

The windows had been smashed and offered a possible escape route, but glass remained and it was dangerous; the only viable exit was the solitary doorway. David Singh now manoeuvred his body around so that he stood in front of the young lady, his overweight body pushing her back against the wall.

"It's ok, dear. I'll look after you. Why don't you come to me?"

Smiling his greasy, insincere smile, he held out his arms inviting her for an embrace. Horrified, and having only escaped one predator for another, she backed away.

"It's ok dear, don't be afraid. Tell me, did the Englishman…" he paused, thinking how best to phrase the question. "Did he, you know, dear, did he…?"

Minder continued to shuffle backwards. She hadn't been too badly affected by the summer humidity, but now sweat dripped down her sari and her heartbeat increased.

With his left hand David Singh joined his index finger to his thumb, making a circle; then he pushed his index finger from his right hand in and out of the circle. "Well? Did he?"

Finally the frightened lady made for the doorway but David Singh pinned her back against the wall. Upon her pretty face she could feel David Singh's odorous breath.

"Don't be afraid. There's nothing to be afraid of. It's natural. Everyone does it, even your father did it at least once, I think; unless your mother was playing away."

He winked at her which was pointless as it was nearly pitch black. The petrified young lady looked to move away but she was blocked by the master's arms and his oversized, large belly which now glued her to the stone wall. She wanted to scream, but who would hear her in this deserted house and deserted village? With nothing but dry farms and no-one and nothing save for a few lost cattle wandering aimlessly, what hope did she have? In her panic she began hyper-ventilating.

"Just relax dear. You'll enjoy it. Maybe not the first time, but it gets easier and easier. We'll practice lots and lots."

She turned her head away so as to avoid his tongue being forced down her throat, but she was unable to avoid his slobbering kisses upon her neck.

"No, please don't. Please…"

He forced her back against the wall and attempted to stab his crotch into her. "How about that?"

"Please, please don't…" Tears ran down her cheeks.

"What about those breasts then? You know, I'm a great fan of those…"

He placed his right hand over her left breast and squeezed it, rubbing his palm over her nipple and then gently pinching it. "Isn't that marvellous?"

"Please stop.... Please…"

David Singh giggled as he licked her neck, inadvertently tasting the salt form her tears which he unceremoniously spat out onto the floor. Minder futilely struggled, though there was part of her which told her simply to accept her fate; she was powerless against this beast and was in the hands of the gods. As he groped, fondled, prodded and licked, she closed her eyes and prayed.

"Arrggghhhh! My back!"

He'd been having back pains for a while, and this was the worst time for it to give way. David Singh released his victim and placed his hands across his lower back, which he attempted to straighten. Minder looked to take the opportunity to escape but she was held even tighter against the wall by the master's protruding stomach now that he was arching his back.

"Bloody bastard," quipped he to the fan; for the late night humidity coupled with the exercise he was just about to do had brought a considerable patch of sweat to his back. He wiped his hands on Minder's sari. Though clearly in pain, the rapist was not too be deterred.

"Never mind, there's other things we can do."

Gripping her platted hair tight, he pushed her head down with his sweaty hand so that she was kneeling before his crotch. As he felt for his penis the stricken lady could only beg in between her sobs.

"Please... Please... Please... Don't make me do it... Please stop it... I beg you... Think of my father..."

"That's the last thing I want to think of right now."

He managed to free his penis and hold it in front of Minder's mouth. She turned her head away with a strong urge to vomit, for the stench was unbearable and nothing like anything she had ever known; even the latrines were more fragrant. David Singh gripped her hair tighter so that she was unable to turn away, but he struggled to convince her to open her mouth and allow his little, smelly sausage inside.

"Come on, be a good girl," he muttered through gritted teeth, for the pain in his back was not subsiding. "Arrrggghhhh!"

Another sharp pain went surging through his back. The master placed one hand over the pain and felt the sweat pouring down his back.

"Arrrrggghhhh! What the bloody hell?"

And then he knew he wasn't coated in sweat, but in blood.

"Arrrggggghhhh!"

He released his grip and fell to his knees, so that he faced Minder, who looked on in bafflement and shock. David Singh fell backwards so that he lay on his back, facing the ceiling fan and with his limp, penis hanging out. As his vision blurred he could just about make out a figure of a man holding what looked to be a dagger. He slowly extracted his final breaths.

"I'm being so sorry, Brigadier-General, Sir. I was only trying to looking after her for you... You know, just breaking her in for you... Please... forgiving... me..."

The Brigadier-General lent forward and took Minder by the hand; she pulled it back but could not escape his grip. Again she began remonstrating, screaming, kicking out, cursing, until she got into the moonlight. Through her tears she saw that the hand that held hers belonged not to the strange foreigner, but to her father.

Afghanistan 2012

On an American military base, in an empty room are an Afghani nomad and British soldier. The Afghani is dressed in traditional dress complete with sandals and beard. He has short, dark, unkempt hair and sports a smart turban. He sits in the centre of the room on a chair, which is the only item of furniture. Above the man is a fan which gives some respite from the thick, humid desert heat. There is a solitary window which allows for light. The British soldier, a thin, lanky, clean shaven man keeps guard. He is slight in stature and well spoken. Both men seem to be in good spirits.

TERRORIST
Hello. What's your name?

POODLE
Private Poodle. And you?

TERRORIST
Ali Abdulaziz Abdullah Ahmed Awar Al-Alqadi, aka Evil Terrorist. But my friends call me George. Nice to meet you.

POODLE
Likewise.

TERRORIST
Will you get out of our country?

POODLE
No.

TERRORSIT
I can offer you many wives and a great herd of camels.

POODLE
No, it's quite alright. You keep your camels.

TERRORIST
Do you want sheep instead? You like sheep, don't you?

POODLE
No, I don't want anything.

TERRORIST
You want the oil.

POODLE
Well, maybe…

TERRORSIT
Maybe yes.

POODLE
Oil is more valuable than camels or sheep.

TERRORIST
You speak in truths. Let me ask you this: When you have an uninvited guest in your house, an intruder, what do you do?

POODLE
Well, I don't blow myself up to smithereens just to get him out; that's naughty. I would call the police.

TERRORIST
And the police in this case are…

POODLE

Daddy.

TERRORIST
What the hell? *Daddy?*

POODLE
Yes, *Daddy*. What Daddy tells us to do we have to do it, don't we? Or else we'd end up in trouble, wouldn't we? And we don't what that now, do we?

TERRORIST
You're a fucking idiot! I'm talking about America being the world's policeman. I don't know what your problem is, talking about... *Daddy!*

POODLE
Well, metaphorically speaking America is Daddy.

TERRORIST
Not my fucking daddy.

POODLE
Actually I'm talking about Lieutenant Budding Imperialist. He'll be ever so cross when he comes.

TERRORIST
Why don't you convert to our side? Join us. We'll give you the biggest farm in all of Afghanistan.

POODLE
No, thank you. That's awfully kind but daddy says never accept gifts from brown people.

TERRORIST
Killing is wrong, isn't it? Wouldn't you say?

POODLE
Daddy says it's ok if it gets you lots of oil and it's only brown people who die.

TERRORIST
To hell with Daddy! I curse his mother and spit in his face!

POODLE
Daddy says there is no mummy.

TERRORIST
Fuck your mummy!

POODLE
How dare you! You'll pay once I tell the Lieutenant what you said about his parentage.

TERRORIST
Listen, say one day you didn't do as your daddy told you. What would happen?

POODLE
He'd be jolly cross and I imagine that he would not talk to me for a long while; and he'd talk to everybody else, especially the people who don't like me, and he'd cause trouble for me.

TERRORIST
I see. Do you have many enemies?

POODLE
Well, not so much enemies as competitors. You see, old boy, this business of being a world power is very

competitive. Everyone wants to be one nowadays; it's all the rage.

From his backside Evil Terrorist pulls a crumpled piece of paper.

TERRORIST
Look! Look what I've got! A note from your daddy!

POODLE *(excited)*
Really? What does it say? Read it! Read it!

TERRORIST
It says: To my fellow infidels, my sons, daughters, and all of my children…

POODLE
I'm the most important child.

TERRORIST
…Daddy orders you to pack your bags and go home immediately. Leave these peaceful jihadists to live their tranquil way of life. We'll talk later. Goodbye. And don't forget to tip Ali Abdulaziz Abdullah Ahmed Awar Al-Alqadi, aka Evil Terrorist.

POODLE
No! Daddy wouldn't just do that. He never tips people.

TERRORIST
Well, there's a first time for everything.

POODLE
I guess so. I wish he'd have told me first. He's always doing things and not telling me.

41

TERRORIST
Well, it's been nice knowing you...

POODLE
Yes, sorry it was so short. You know, I'm going to miss eating Keshari, and I had some great vine leaves here.

TERRORIST
Don't worry, you can get everything at Tesco's. They're doing two for three at the moment.

POODLE
Really? Well I'll have a bit of that.

TERRORIST
Yes, why don't you? Do you want some help packing?

POODLE
No, I'm quite alright. Besides, I don't want you to see the porn mags I've been stashing. I know you're a bit sensitive about tits and things. Anyone would think you're a homosexual.

TERRORIST
What? On your mother's grave I break wind, and then I urinate and finally I defecate! For that insult I kill you.

POODLE
I was only joking old boy. Can one not take a joke?

TERRORIST
No, one cannot take a fucking joke!

A stout man enters the room. His uniform is pristine and well-decorated. His cap is pulled over his eyes barely revealing them. He speaks in a thick Southern drawl.

IMPERIALIST
Say, what's all this bullshit fuss goin' on?

POODLE
Daddy!

IMPERIALIST
That's an awful lot of racket comin' from here.

POODLE
Oh, Daddy, I'm so pleased to see you!

IMPERIALIST
Shut your hole boy! The back of my hand'll be the next thing you see. Now then, Mr Evil Terrorist, I want your oil, and there's nothing you can do about it.

TERRORIST
I will kill you.

IMPERIALIST
That may be so, but I'll sure kill you first.

TERRORIST
I'll kill all your family and your friends.

IMPERIALIST
Well, I'll just do likewise. I'll kill all your family and friends before they were born. How about that?

TERRORIST
That's genius; you can travel in time?

IMPERIALIST
Well, not quite. But, all the same, I'm gonna wire your testicles up to some live wires and ram this electronically charged baton up your ass.

TERRORIST
Ah, but you can't.

IMPERIALIST
Can and sure will. See how you like that.

TERRORIST
But I confess.

IMPERIALIST
What?

TERRORIST
I confess everything. So there's no need to wire anything up to my testicles.

IMPERIALIST
But you can't! You can't confess!

TERORIST
Can and sure will. In fact, I believe I just have.

IMPERIALIST
Son of a… But I wanted to strip you naked and put a black hood on your head and humiliate you, just for my own gratification, you understand? The photos don't really do anything, I need the real thing.

TERRORIST
Well, there's no need. I confess everything. I did it.
I did everything.

IMPERIALIST
You son of a… That's not fair! My boys were gonna
whoop your ass… and one of them was gonna penetrate
it, too.

TERRORIST
Well, it's completely unnecessary as I confess to
everything.

IMPERIALIST
Even to plotting to kill all the leaders of the free
world at the same time?

TERRORIST
What? Are you mad?

IMPERIALIST
Awesome! Drop your pants and where are those live
wires?

TERRORIST
Erm… I mean, of course, of course I plotted to kill
all the leaders of the free world. Who wouldn't?

IMPERIALIST
Damn it! It ain't fair!

POODLE
Strike him, Daddy!

TERRORIST

Shut the fuck up boy, or I'll strike your ass! So, you confess, Evil Terrorist. Tell me, firstly, where did you get your arms?

TERRORIST
I was born with them. They came with my legs.

IMPERIALIST
Hand me those wires....

TERRORIST
Ah, you mean weapons? Sorry, my English isn't so proficient; I only studied at Eton then Oxford. I bought them off some guy called Jamal.

IMPERIALIST
Where is he, this evil Jamal dude?

TERRORIST
He's dead.

IMPERIALIST
See that, boy. That's the beauty of American technological and militaristic precision. Air strikes!

TERRORIST
No, he had a cardiac arrest. Apparently he had a predilection towards fried foods.

IMPERIALIST
Did he say where he got his arms?

TERRORIST
He was born with them...

IMPERIALIST

Hand me those wires…

TERRORIST
Ah, I mean he got them off his mate who lives in a cave somewhere.

IMPERIALIST
Damn those caves! We've been bombing those evil caves for some time now. God damn caves! Motherfuckers! I hate them! They'll never defeat the might of the American army! Never!

TERRORIST
Yes, I agree. Can I go home now?

IMPERIALIST
Not until you tell me where those arms came from.

TERRORIST
Whose arms?

IMPERIALIST
Not *whose* arms, *which* arms.

TERRORIST
Which arms?

IMPERIALIST
Yes, which arms.

TERRORIST
No, I'm asking you; which arms are you talking about?

IMPERIALIST
This Jamal terrorist; his arms.

TERRORIST
Oh, he was born with them, they came with...

IMPERIALIST
What the… Boy!

TERRORIST
Oh, I see… Well, Jamal is dead, so I don't know.

IMPERIALIST
Where was this terrorist Jamal from?

TERRORIST
From a cave. But I think he said his great, great, great grandfather had some Iranian blood in him.

IMPERIALIST
Iran! So it's the Iranians?

TERRORIST
Well, no…

IMPERIALIST
Of course it is. Damn those evil Iranians, sitting on all those natural resources.

TERRORIST *(gets up to leave)*
Well, it's been a pleasure knowing you…

IMPERIALIST *(pushes Terrorist back down)*
Sit your ass down! Now then, tell me who was involved in the plot?

TERRORIST
My uncle Amed, who is dead. Uncle Abddullah,
who is dead; uncle Hassan, who is dead; Uncle
Hussein, who is dead; Uncle Ali, who is missing but
presumed dead; Uncle Abdurrahman, who is dead;
Uncle Saad, who is dead; Uncle Raed, who is dead;
Uncle Ibrahim, who is dead; and Uncle Majed, who is
nearly dead.

IMPERIALIST
Yep, he's next door getting a good old fashioned
beating. He'll be dead soon. And so will you be if you
don't tell us everything.

TERRORIST
I'm telling you! I'm telling you!

IMPERIALIST
Then tell me this: What's the meaning of life?

TERRORIST
To live shallow, materialistic lives where we will
always remain unfulfilled as we futilely pursue wealth?

IMPERIALIST
Close, but no cigar. Now show me those testicles
and switch to maximum voltage.

TERRORIST
That's not fair! You didn't say I had to answer deep
philosophical questions that man has been pondering
for thousands of years and still found no answer to.

IMPERIALIST
I ain't gotta tell ya nothin' I don't wanna. Now drop
your pants!

TERRORIST
No, you must give me time to answer such a complicated question.

IMPERIALIST
There ain't no time you asshole. We're fightin' a god damn war!

TERRORIST
In that case, surely the meaning of life lays hidden in the twelve Emerald Tablets of Thoth, an esoteric knowledge bequeathed tens of thousands of years ago by a former Atlantean, informing mankind about the keys and mysteries to life.

IMPERIALIST
What the fuck are you goin' on about?

TERRORIST
Erm… I mean the meaning of life is to extract oil, gas and other natural resources from our planet and then make billions of dollars exploiting them. And killing people whilst doing so?

IMPERIALIST
God damn! How the hell did you know? Son of a…

POODLE
Daddy, can I go to the toilet?

IMPERIALIST
Shut up, boy. I told ya, an' I ain't tellin' ya again.

POODLE
What did you tell me?

IMPERIALIST
I already told ya, so I ain't telling ya again.

POODLE
But I've forgotten, Daddy.

IMPERIALIST
Shut up, boy. Now you just stand there and pee your pants, or else you ain't never gone learn. As for you, Umbongo Awbongo....

TERRORIST
Actually, my name's Ali Abdulaziz Abdullah Ahmed Awar Al-Alqadi, aka Evil Terrorist. But my friends call me George.

IMPERIALIST
Well, I ain't gonna be callin' ya that 'cos ya ain't no friend o' mine. Then again, George sure is a lot easier than Bong Bongo, or whatever your bullshit name is.

TERRORIST
Bongo Bongo is just fine.

IMPERIALIST
Now tell me, you evil terrorist, who conjured this plot?

TERRORIST
Well, you see after a couple of bombs fell on the village, killing my entire family apart from my Uncle Majed...

IMPERIALIST

Ah, yes, he's still next door getting his ass rammed with electricity, like you'll be doing soon unless you tell me the god damn truth!

TERRORIST
I'm telling you! I'm telling you! My Uncle Majed decided there was nothing left to do but seek revenge on the pilots who dropped the bomb killing our family, livestock, cattle and crops. So he bought a surface-to-air missile from this guy called Jamal, in a cave.

IMPERIALIST
God damn Iranians!

TERRORIST
It turned out to be a giant water melon and not a surface-to-air missile at all. My Uncle Majed is a bit docile.

IMPERIALIST
Was.

TERRORIST
I'm sorry?

IMPERIALIST
Was a bit docile, your majic uncle. He's dead; your last remaining family member.

TERRORIST
Oh, well. Another one bites the dust.

IMPERIALIST
Carry on your story.

TERRORIST
Well, after he'd got ripped off, that's when the
American soldiers came. They saw the giant
watermelon; then once they had beaten, assaulted,
sexually assaulted, humiliated and mocked us, they
arrested us and charged us with killing our own family.

IMPERIALIST
Hold on a minute, what's that smell?

TERRORIST
Yes, I can smell it too. It's gas.

IMPERIALIST
You've got chemicals weapons up your ass? Search
him, boy!

TERRORIST
No! No! It's not me. It's your son.

POODLE
Daddy, I've soiled myself.

IMPERIALIST
What the...? I thought you needed a number one,
not a number two! You were supposed to *piss* your
pants, not *shit* your pants! Gad damn asshole! Can't do
nothing right!

POODLE
Sorry, Daddy.

IMPERIALIST
Get outta here before I kick your god damn shit-
ridden ass! Go wipe your crack! Stoo-pid
motherfucker!

[Captain Poodle exits the room]

What is it with these god damn poodles?

TERRORIST
Yes, I agree. And the stench they leave behind.

IMPERIALIST
They're still better than you, because they're obedient and loyal. They let us do as we like and they do as we say. And they don't try to kill us.

TERRORIST
You mean they bend over and let you bum them while we fight for our freedom?

IMPERIALIST
Something like that. Now, Umbongo, tell me one more thing.

TERRORIST
It'd be a pleasure.

IMPERIALIST
When you were plotting to kill all the leaders of the free world, you must have created some cells somewhere.

TERRORIST
Cells? Yes, we have hundreds.

IMPERIALIST
Hundreds?

TERRORIST

No, thousands…

IMPERIALIST
Thousands?

TERRORIST
Who knows? Millions?

IMPERIALIST
What the…? You've got millions of cells all over the world?

TERRORIST
No, just in my body.

IMPERIALIST
In your body? What the…? Are you some kind of asshole? Boy! Get back in here when you're done wiping your ass and get me some electric wires and that baton.

TERRORIST
Oh, you mean terrorist cells. No, we never got beyond mistakenly purchasing a giant watermelon.

IMPERIALIST
I know you're lying.

TERRORIST
It's the only time I've really told the truth; you see, we never plotted to kill…

IMPERIALIST
Boy! Get your ass in here now and get me some highly charged wires!

[Captain Poodle re-enters]

TERRORIST
Oh, yes, cells, of course. There was only one.

IMPERIALIST
Where was it? And answer the question as if your life depends on it.

TERRORIST
That's not difficult. The terrorist cell was in London.

IMPERIALIST
London? You mean, London, Ohio? Or London, Oregon?

TERRORIST
No...

IMPERIALIST
London, Arkansas?

TERRORIST
No, it's...

IMPERIALIST
Don't tell me! Is it London, Kentucky? How about London, West Virginia?

TERRORIST
No, no, I'm not referring to the London that's in the USA...

IMPERIALIST

You mean there's a London outside of the US? Let me see... You mean... It must be London, Ontario?

TERRORIST
No, it's not the London that's in Canada either.

IMPERIALIST
Let me guess! Don't tell me.... Is it the London that's in Belize?

TERRORIST
Nope.

IMPERIALIST
The London that's in Kiribati?

TERRORIST
Not even close.

IMPERIALIST
God damn! It must be the London in Equatorial Guinea?

TERRORIST
Nope.

IMPERIALIST
No? Don't tell me! Don't tell me... It's gotta be London in Limpopo?

TERRORIST
Afraid not.

IMPERIALIST
Well, all that's left is London in Mpumalanga.

TERRORIST
Well it ain't there.

IMPERIALIST
God damn! Motherfucker! Wait a minute... I used to know a dirty little porn star called London. You ain't talking about her are ya?

TERRORIST
Nope. It's definitely a city and not a woman who performs erotic acts in front of a video camera in order to receive monetary gain.

IMPERIALIST
To hell with it! Ok, damn it! I give in! Tell me!

TERRORIST
But you said not to.

IMPERIALIST
Boy...

TERRORIST
Ok... It's London, England.

IMPERIALIST
England? What the fuck's that?

TERORIST
It's a country.

IMPERIALIST
There ain't no god damn country called Eng-what?

TERRORIST
England. It's where your dog comes from.

IMPERIALIST
Is that right, boy?

POODLE
Yes, Daddy. I'm also from London, England.

IMPERIALIST
But you're British, you asshole!

POODLE
Yes, Daddy. But I'm also English. You see the British Isles is made up of three countries, four if you include Northern Ireland, though they're not actually part of the isles as technically and geographically they're part of a separate island, which would be Ireland, but all that's a bit sensitive. Anyway, they are still part of the United Kingdom and...

IMPERIALIST
Shut your god damn mouth! No one gives a shit about your bullshit isles. Anyway, Umbongo, let's get back to the point; what about the cell?

TERRORIST
Ah, yes. It was called Tesco's.

IMPERIALIST
Tesco's?

TERRORIST
Yes, if you go to England...

IMPERIALIST
I don't know of no place called Ass-land.

TERRORIST
I mean go to Britain; if you go to Britain you'll see signs of us everywhere.

IMPERIALIST
Where can I find these Tesco's terrorists?

TERRORIST
They're all over London.

IMPERIALIST
Is that London, Ohio? Or London, Oregon? London, Arkansas? Or London, Kentucky? How about London, West Virginia?

TERRORIST
No… It's London, England.

IMPERIALIST
Now stop makin' up these fictional countries or Daddy's 'bout to get real angry.

TERRORIST
I mean London in Britain; Tesco's are everywhere.

IMPERIALIST
And how can I recognize a Tesco jihadist?

TERRORIST
They wear these awfully cheap, blue and black checked shirts and dark trousers with dark shoes; and they normally get paid minimum wage.

IMPERIALIST
And where do they live?

TERRORIST
In giant buildings, the size of a warehouse with enormous signs on them.

IMPERIALIST
And what do these enormous signs say?

TERRORIST
Tesco's.

IMPERIALIST
I see...

POODLE
Daddy! Daddy! He's tricking you. Tesco's a supermar...

IMPERIALIST
Shut your god damn hole, boy! You're about as much use as a penis in a monastery.

POODLE
But he's making a fool of you, Daddy.

IMPERIALIST
You're the only fool here, god damn asshole! Now shut the fuck up! As for you, we're pretty much done.

TERRORIST
Well, that wasn't too bad. Have a nice day then.

IMPERIALIST
Wait a minute. You ain't goin' nowhere.

TERRORIST
I thought we were done.

IMPERIALIST
We are. But you ain't.

TERRORIST
What? But I've cooperated and told you everything you wanted to hear.

IMPERIAIST
Yep, and now your sorry ass is gonna have to go to court and stand trial for being an evil terrorist and plotting to kill everyone in the world.

TERRORIST
It's *everyone* now, is it?

IMPERIALIST
Yep.

TERRORIST
You don't have much evidence.

IMPERIALIST
We've got your confession.

TERRORIST
Well, I might say it was a false confession made under duress.

IMPERIALIST
Don't matter if you do, 'cos we got your giant watermelon as well!

TERRORIST
Fair enough, I suppose. I guess I'll have to prepare my own defence?

IMPERIALIST
Yep, and you've got a couple of years to prepare it.

TERRORIST
What? I thought the American courts were efficient and not filled with corruption and backlog like ours?

IMPERIALIST
That's right, but you're goin' to Guantanamo.

TERRORIST
Guantanamo?

IMPERIALIST
Yep, and by the time your trial comes round you ain't even gonna know your own name.

TERRORIST
Oh well. Just as well I suppose. It's probably better that way.

IMPERIALIST
You've got one more chance to have your testicles wired up to some highly charged electrical wires.

TERRORIST
If I do, then do I have to still go to Guantanamo?

IMPERIALIST
Of course not.

TERORIST
Well, that's ok then. I'll pass. I'll just go straight to Guantanamo.

IMPERIAIST
What? Well you can have your testicles wired up and still go to Guantanamo.

TERORIST
No, I'll just go straight to Guantanamo. I've always wanted to go abroad.

IMPERIALIST
You seem awfully relaxed.

TERRORIST
Well, it's all just God's will.

IMPERIALIST
Whatever. Well, good luck with the trial Umbongo.

TERRORIST
And good luck with killing more people, amongst whom are many, if not mostly, innocents.

IMPERIALIST
That shouldn't be a problem.

TERRORIST *[gets up to leave]*
Do you mind if I kick your dog on my way out.

IMPERIALIST
Well, I guess you have been cooperative, even if you didn't let me wire up your testicles. Sure, be my guest.

POODLE
But Daddy…

Eastern Nepal
March 2006

I

"Namaste," smiled the young man, clasping his hands together and bowing his head deferentially, only to be met by a cold and authoritative voice.

"Who's that?" She raised her rifle.

From undercover of moonlight and via a squint (it was pitch black - electricity hadn't yet reached the countryside) he could just about make out a blue-grey uniform adorned by a five-foot tall revolutionary; she clutched a weapon aimed at his head. He started; the shock stunning him into silence. Devendra lowered her cap over her forehead and raised her neckerchief above her mouth so it sat on her nose, leaving only a pair of dark, severe eyes on show; eyes that defied her thirty years; eyes that carried the look of a battle-hardened warrior, eyes that intimidated with a deadly, piercing stare; eyes that warned against any tomfoolery; eyes that could tell a hundred murderous stories.

"Raise your hands so I can see them. What's your business here?"

The fear that gripped Annuj now paralysed him; while he was able to lift his hands above his head, he was unable to put his tongue into operation.

"Speak!" forcefully commanded Devendra, like that of an overly strict headmistress, causing Annuj to jump, his eyes to swell with tears and his bladder to emit a little liquid. "Who are you? What's your business here? Speak or I'll shoot; don't think I won't."

Understanding that his life was at a premature end, the teenager fell to his knees, both of which subsequently released a steady trickle of blood, attracting mosquitoes as they landed upon sharp stones which littered the dirt track.

"Please don't kill me," he begged pathetically, with eyes about to let rip a flood of water.

Witnessing such a pathetic figure before her, with his saddened eyes, Devendra, for the first time in a long, long time, felt something she had long forgotten, an emotion that had become as extinct as decency and democracy: sympathy. Her eyes softened.

Noting the transformation, the young man almost relaxed – rather, he started to breathe again. Having adjusted to the nocturnal light he now noticed the beauty in her dark, oval eyes – eyes which opened wide and invited him inside; eyes that told of an enigma; eyes which told of a human behind the beast of a soldier; eyes that perpetrated the myth that all these revolutionaries were, as his father had put it, 'mindless, filthy things'. Perhaps she would spare him after all.

"You're beautiful," he whispered aloud, causing further confusion inside the woman's mind; for it had been many, many years since she had heard any quixotic utterances. Had there not been a time when she had felt love? Had not a beloved once wrapped her in a tender embrace and whispered those words so sweetly and delicately in her ear? Was there not an occasion when laughter, joy and innocence had once been prevalent in her life?

She came back to her senses; her guard had been dropped; emotions were for the weak. Again, the cold, hard stare.

"Chauvinist! What's your business here? Speak or I'll shoot you right in the head!" As if to confirm this she rested the butt of the rifle on her shoulder and took aim. A barrage of barely coherent words came from Annuj.

"I'm here, with parents... my parents. We're only here... for a weekend. We come here... come here... sometimes. I was just... going out... walking. I like the clean... the clean... country air... even though the mosquitoes are really bad out here. But my father is... he is so boring and terrible I'd rather... get eaten by... by mosquitoes..."

"Where are you from?"

"Kathmandu."

The place clearly evoked a memory in her mind, for she now looked at Annuj with some interest. Her mind again began to drift to some distant memory, to a time and place that had long ceased to exist in her world; a time and place which she had spent so long running from. Just as a man had once whispered sweet nothings to her, so too had Kathmandu. There she had led a sweet life at first, as childhood should be; but a bitter end to her time in the capital and a harsh introduction into adulthood brought about the end of her innocence. She rapidly quashed her memory, crushing it just as the tanks of the monarchy did its people.

"What are you doing here?"

"My family often come here at the weekend. They own a house not too far away."

"Typical bourgeois swine."

"Are you a revolutionary?"

She spoke as a great orator would have; her conviction was plain to see. "I am here to liberate the people of Nepal from the tyranny of our corrupt, self-serving leaders. I am fighting against the oppression we are subjected to by our cruel masters. I am fighting to reclaim our country for the masses, for the people who sweat blood, who are exploited and abused for the profit of this despotic tyranny we call our monarchy. Let our kings and queens tremble at our communist revolution. The proletarians have nothing to lose but their chains. We have a country to win. We fight for a better Nepal. We die to liberate our country and if that means we sacrifice ourselves, then so be it. As long as we remain united, they can do nothing, for we are a million strong, and to defeat us they must kill each and every one of us."

Annuj, heavy with sweat from the close late evening heat, fluctuated between fear and fascination, for the woman attracted a desire within him hitherto unknown. True, he was petrified, after all, the Maoist guerrillas were well known to all for their ferocity; he didn't doubt that she would kill him, particularly as he was a class enemy – he oozed middle-class - his well-kept hair; his smooth, clean skin; his spotless, Western style clothing; his educated accent. Yet he was unable to deny his attraction to the revolutionary, to the short woman who showed more spirit than anyone he had ever known, even his over exuberant father. This attraction kept him sane in an otherwise hopeless situation. Could there be such a thing as love at first sight?

"I can help."

Devendra gave a scornful laugh.

"Please, let me help the cause."

"You? A bourgeois pig! I bet you live in a mansion in Kathmandu with a hundred servants. You take weekend breaks in the country and you sound as though you have a plum up your bum, no doubt thanks to the finest education your parents have afforded. What can *you* offer the revolution?"

"I can help you, I really can."

"Let me see your palms."

The man lowered his hands and turned them over so Devendra could inspect them in the moonlight. She lightly touched them, causing a sensation to run down Annuj's spine and make him tingle all over.

"As I thought: never done a day's work in your life."

He was desperate to pull down her neckerchief and plant a kiss on her lips, on her neck, to smother her all over with his kisses. He had never seen a naked woman before, but now, more than at any time before, he wanted to strip her, to ravish her, to taste her and to be tasted. He had no experience of women any more than he had experience of life – the two concepts totally alien to him, but both of which he desperately longed for.

"Let me come with you. *Please*. I want to help. I hate our monarchy just as you do. I see the excessiveness of the rich every day – my family is part of that culture of greed – and so am I, but I long to be different. On the train I've seen the faces of the poor and the hungry, the emaciated and starved; and I feel shame, because I'm part of those who perpetuate such misery. Each night my family eat a feast that would feed a hundred; in a day they spend more than most people do in a year. If you could see how shallow they are, the things that worry them, so superficial, such wretched extravagance. Let me join you."

Annuj had not realised that he was so politically aware; at best he opted to be indifferent about politics, choosing to be blind to the suffering and pretending not to hear the cries of anguish or the stench of disease. But had this spirited young lady sparked off a latent revolutionary zeal inside of him? Or was it nothing more than the young man's hormones taking control of his mind?

"Fool! What can you bring the struggle other than harm? Your family will track down their precious boy and in the process slaughter us all. Haven't we suffered enough? And by your foolery we will suffer more."

"But you're so beautiful. I have never seen eyes like yours before. Please, lower your mask so I can see your lips; I bet they are as beautiful as your eyes; so... how do I put it? Enigmatic."

Devendra relaxed her rifle and ordered the young man to stand and again raise his hands. Her dilemma was that should she release him, he may tell others, namely the military or the police, of her whereabouts and that the army would find the clandestine camp. On the other hand, if she were to shoot him, or take him back with her, then undoubtedly his family would send a search party to find him and again it would risk the camp.

She sighed, sweat running down her brow from the awful humid heat. He continued to look at her with a mixture of awe and melancholy. It had been so long since she had trusted anyone outside of the guerrillas, yet his eyes told her he was genuine. His eyes told her he, too, just as herself, was unhappy. For the first time Devendra noticed that he was a handsome young man: broad shoulders, thick lips, dark round eyes and a strong physique. Yes, he was good looking; she wondered what it would be like if she let him, a fledgling teenager, kiss her.

"Annuj! Annuj! Where are you? Everyone's waiting for you. Your father's going crazy with worry. Annuj, what are you doing with your hands in the air?"

There was no need to reply as the torch the servant held shone upon the Maoist guerrilla. His jaw dropped to the floor and his eyes opened wide; next, in a panic, he reached for his rifle which was slung across his back.

"No, Baja! It's fine."

But for Baja it wasn't fine; he would be held responsible for any harm that came to the boy. As he attempted to grip his rifle he dropped the torch, handing the advantage to Devendra, whose night-time vision had developed well with years of nocturnal fighting.

72

"Leave your gun," commanded she.

The servant looked at her with revulsion. "You bloody, mindless, filthy thing!" He raised his rifle and by the time he had taken aim a bullet had entered and left his head.

"Baja!"

Annuj ran over to the corpse whose blood rapidly attracted a swarm of mosquitoes. The young man rested his bloodied knees besides the man who had been more of a father to him than his own father. He placed his well-kept hands on the holes in Baja's head to stem the blood; realising it was futile, he broke down.

Watching the young man sob pulled her heart strings, which was unusual, for she never felt sympathy for her victims. Yet, hadn't she, too, once, felt such pain? Was there not an occasion where she had cried, wailed, mourning a loss? Buried in her memory there were emotions that Annuj was displaying; emotions that came flooding back with the memories of her youth in Kathmandu; emotions and memories, intertwined, that ripped out her heart.

Seized by a fit of rage, the young man grabbed Baja's rifle.

"No!" shouted Devendra, whose tears mingled with her sweat.

Just as his servant, Annuj was dead before he could even take aim; his body slumped over the man who had cared for him since he was born.

Back to playing the cold, hardened and ruthless soldier, the petite revolutionary pulled the two bodies on to the side of the road, covering them with leaves and branches. She made her way back to the camp, abandoning her mission to lay dynamite on the train track, instead seized by an urgency to inform her camp of what had happened so that they could move on before the reprisals.

As she steadily made her way back through the night-time humidity, the image of the two men lying dead replayed over and over in her mind. She couldn't help but weep; only she knew not why.

II

"Isn't she done yet?"

The voice was cold and authoritative, so too was it deep and hoarse. Devendra was in far too much pain to reply; instead the nurse did so for her.

"Please, be patient, Sir. It won't be much longer."

Gyanendra had lost his patience long ago.

It was winter and the snow from the Himalayas could be felt from the Easterly wind. He was keen to leave the servants' quarters and get back to the warmth of his lavish mansion; there he had much more pressing matters to see to. He had companies to run, companies to start up, companies to close down; important people to see, accounts to manage, and that kind of thing. There were never enough hours in the day for the serial entrepreneur, and this was the last thing the plump man needed.

"Push!" encouraged the midwife. "You're almost there!"

While the teenage Devendra huffed and heaved, the much older man turned his gaze to the ceiling, inspecting its cracks. He had never believed that his liaison with the maid would cause him so much trouble, after all, his liaisons with the other maids were always forgotten as soon as they were started. But as yet, he hoped that there may well be a silver lining to this noisy cloud.

He spat on his finger tips and patted down his perfect parting.

"Squeeze my hand, dear... It's ok... Deep breaths... Come on..."

75

The sight of the girl covered in sweat, losing blood and screaming with pain was in stark contrast to the young beauty he had enticed into his bedroom with his sleazy charm and false promises. Hard to believe it was the same person, thought Gyanendra, finding yet more hairline fractures in the ceiling.

"I can see the head! You're almost there! Come on, dear! Push! Push!"

Where his deceased wife had failed him, and all the hussies since, perhaps this one could succeed. More than anything he wanted a son; a son to whom he could bequeath his empire; a son who would carry the family name on into eternity; a son who would continue his family line; a true heir to a true king.

"Almost, dear! Come on! Push!"

He had a daughter; his wife was capable of that much. But what value of something so second-class? Why invest so heavily in something which had so little return? His daughter was perhaps destined for some good things: she had a good education awaiting her from the best teachers and the dearest schools, and she would have opportunities for high-profile work. At the end of the day, though, she would leave to be part of another family, deserting her ageing father, leaving him alone with only his servants, maids, waiters, doormen, chauffeurs, cleaners and whores. He shuddered at the thought of his lonely old age.

An almighty cry from the fifteen year old drew Gyanendra's attention away from the dilapidated ceiling to the sweat covered new mother. The crying of a new-born could be heard. The midwife cut the umbilical cord and wrapped the delicate baby in a soft, red blanket, then handed him over to his exhausted mother, worn from a laborious labour and excruciating birth.

Upon seeing the thing that had grown inside her for the past eight and a half months and which had come out into the world so stubbornly and cumbersomely, Devendra smiled a magical smile. As she panted heavily the midwife placed the baby in her arms and wiped her brow, moving the hairs that had become glued to her face with sweat.

The teenager shook her head in disbelief, unable to fathom the miracle; overcome with emotion and drained she began weeping. Her life until then hadn't been so bad; she quite enjoyed her menial tasks: sweeping floors, scrubbing dishes, picking fruit, cooking dinners, washing pots; the only part she truly despised was having to sleep with the master. This she did with closed eyes while dreaming she was in far-away places like America, which had rivers, mountains, gold fields, and where everyone was free. But nothing compared to what had just happened. She held the baby upon her breast and looked deep into his eyes. With the smile on her face becoming permanent, she opened her mouth to speak, but she knew not what to say, so simply she shed tears of joy.

"Well?" Gyanendra asked the midwife.

"Well what?"

"What do you think? The thingy; does it have a..?" He raised his index finger. "Or a..?" He bent the finger to touch his thumb as if making an ok sign.

"It's a boy," the maid told him with some repugnance.

Gyanendra stood for a moment, not expecting the news; he hadn't dared allowed himself to believe for a moment, not after the false alarms and raised expectations with the others. They had been allowed to keep their female off-spring, but, of course, this was different.

He leant forward towards Devendra and placed his hands on the red blanket. Instinctively Devendra moved the child away from him, just as a protective mother does to shield her off-spring from prey. Gyanendra, though, lent over her and took a firmer grip.

"No," whispered Devendra.

He seized the child in his hands.

"No," she whispered a little louder; the highs she had experienced rapidly disintegrating into a low.

He took hold of the baby.

"No..." The sadness distorted her face.

"*No!*" This time she screamed and a flood of tears ran down her twisted and drained features.

As Gyanendra carried his son away from the squalid room to the warmth of his mansion, Devendra lent forward. She would have got out of bed and pursued the master only she was frail and weak.

"Please," she begged and sobbed, holding out her arms. "Please... Please... Please... Let me hold him. Please... A little longer. Please..."

The midwife moved to console her, placing her arms around the fatigued mother and holding her hand. The young Devendra started howling as she lay in her own blood and mucus, shattered, battered and broken. Gyanendra ignored her completely, precariously carrying the child away. He hadn't banked on the girl being such a problem. Something would have to be done; after all, how could he raise his son to be a good aristocrat when the pathetic mother was sullying around after him?

He stopped as he reached the door. "I'll get someone to look at those cracks in the ceiling," he muttered without turning around.

Outside stood the faithful family servant, Baja, dressed as usual in his traditional Nepalese clothing.

"Here," said Gyanendra, handing him the new born. "Take him inside."

"Him?" Baja said with surprise.

"That's right," replied the proud father. "And I'll think I'll name him after my father."

"Annuj?"

"That's right."

"Good choice, Master, good choice."

Eastern Baghdad, Iraq.
July 12th 2007

I

The heavy summer heat beat down upon the unfortunate vehicle, adding to its misery. The van was not too dissimilar from the one the gang used in Scooby-Doo, only it didn't have any hippy flowers or 'The Mystery Machine' colourfully displayed on its side; instead it sported a black colour which gave it more of an A-Team appearance (minus the red stripe).

The aged van, covered in numerous layers of dirt picked up from battered, dusty and dry Baghdad roads, bounced cumbersomely as the driver futilely attempted to avoid the numerous pot-holes and craters that littered its path. Cracks, too, had started to appear in the roads, just as they had in the parched lands in the villages; they threatened to split wide open, like the jaws of a beast opening wide and devouring all before it.

"What's wrong with these people?"

Abdullah, the young, clean shaven, handsome man who always dressed well, posed the question. His clothes were trendy and his hair was well-groomed – short and slick. He tossed the newspaper to Abdo, a much less fashion conscious individual, though no less handsome. Abdo scanned the newspaper with his large brown eyes, skimming the article which had caused his usually passive friend to stir.

"Cho Seung-Hui."

"Who?"

"That's what it says here."

"Doesn't sound American."

"Who said anything about him being American? You're too presumptuous; always cursing the food before you taste it."

"Who grows thorns will reap wounds."

"What's that got to do with anything?"

"Not sure, but it sounds cool."

The two men sat in the back of the rusted vehicle, opposite each other, both perched upon crates, bouncing in rhythm to the beating of the road.

"Cho Seung-Hui. It says here he's Korean."

"Korean?" Abdullah pondered this as he wiped sweat from his brow. The awful heat trapped in the van gave it an oven effect. He let loose another button on his shirt – a Fred Perry shirt he had borrowed from a friend. "I had a Korean girlfriend once."

"Don't bullshit."

"It's true."

Abdo giggled and smiled his warm smile, encouraging his friend to go on. They were indeed good friends, more like brothers, as most people become when embroiled in conflict.

"She was beautiful, you know; really elegant. She wore these really nice trousers, and she had long black hair, really beautiful… Great posture…"

"Great posture? What are you talking about?"

"I'm serious, she had a great posture."

Abdo laughed heartily, his strong features accentuated by his wide grin. He shook his head in disbelief at the fable while Abdullah drifted off to reminisce about his past 'relationship', which, in fact was only a momentary exchange (three minutes to be precise) with a Korean nurse who worked for the UN.

"So what happened? Were you afraid of commitment? Or were you afraid that your Mama was gonna kick your ass for bringing home some random infidel? Or were you just worried her posture was going to fade?"

"It's true, man. I know you don't believe me, but…"

"But nothing; you lie more than George Bush; I don't who to trust more."

Abdullah raised his index finger at his friend, and his friend duly reciprocated with a hand gesture.

"Anyway," said Abdo, returning to the article. "This Korean nutcase just walked through a university and gunned down a load of people; only in America."

Suddenly the van drove over a bump and the occupants all levitated to within inches of banging their heads on the ceiling of the battered vehicle. Abdo turned to the driver.

"Hey, slow down Masala, what are you doing?"

Abdurrahman, aka Masala because of his love of all things spicy, was stressed. He had spent the better part of the day trying to get to the Northern section of the city where he was trying to rebuild his business. He owned a shop which the Taliban had taken over, ransacked and destroyed. Recently the American's had driven them from that part of the city and the retailer was able to reclaim his cloth shop. Only now, as he sought to get the two builders in the back of his van to his shop, he came up against constant road blocks.

He wiped the sweat from his brow and patted down his bushy moustache.

"I think we'll have to turn back; there's no way through. Something must have happened."

"Something's always happening," quipped Abdullah.

"Will we still get paid?" asked Abdo.

Abdurrahman, tired and frustrated, only laughed. The two young men sighed.

The streets were half empty due to the afternoon heat and also the threat of an attack. The Taliban were lurking and you just never knew, particularly when American Apache helicopters were hovering above, circling like black crows. Buildings were splattered with bullet holes, large chunks of debris lay scattered, broken glass, shattered shutters, twisted metal frames, all giving the appearance of scene from a war movie – only this was not a movie.

Masala's countenance altered and he grew visibly enraged; he spotted two young children he knew to belong to a family that lived on his street.

"What the bloody hell are you doing here? Don't you know it's dangerous? Can't you see the bloody helicopters? Get in!"

The two children, a girl and a boy, humbly did as they were told.

"We wanted to play football. I'm Messi and he's Ronaldo."

"I'm Messi. You can be Ronaldo."

"But you're gay, like Ronaldo."

"Shut up! You're the gay one."

"You're both gays!" Masala angrily informed them. "Messi!" He tutted to himself, shaking his head. "You'll both be messy once the Taliban blow your legs off."

The children momentarily fell silent.

"Did you do the English homework?" asked one to the other.

"Are you joking? The school was hit by a bomb last week."

"We still have English class tomorrow."

"No, homework would be inappropriate."

"But the Taliban don't want us to study, so if we don't do the homework then they win."

"What are you talking about? The Taliban can never win because we have the Americans. It's like Real Madrid playing against some crappy team."

"But the crappy team have home advantage."

Masala turned around the corner into what could only be described as a scene befitting hell. Pools of dark red were forming in the parched earth; litter and debris were strewn everywhere as were corpses. The stench of death was fresh. Bodies sprawled around oozing blood, turning the dry dust a crimson red. Whatever had happened, had happened only recently; the crimson dust had yet to settle.

II

Namir laughed at the man carrying the AK47 – the man laughed back.

"What's the joke?"

"I just wonder if I'll get a picture of you shooting or of you being shot."

"And what's the joke?"

"There's no joke."

"So why are you laughing?"

"Because of the joys of life."

The man carrying the AK47 smiled. "The joys of life? You're a crazy bastard! Look, no matter who gets shot, just make sure these pictures get seen around the world. People need to know what's happening."

Namir smiled. "I'll do my best. But I'm just a humble photographer."

"Humble? You're the eyes of the world."

"Yes, but not the brain – and it's the brain that interprets what we see."

"This is no time to be philosophical."

"This is the perfect time to be philosophical."

The two men, who made up a crowd of about a dozen, exchanged curious glances.

See all those people standing down there.

Stay firm. And open the courtyard.

Yeah, roger. I estimate there's probably twenty of them.

There's one.

Yeah, roger.

Hey Bushmaster element, copy on the one-six.

That's a weapon

Yeah.

Hotel two-six. Crazy Horse one-eight.
Copy on the one-six, Bushmaster six-romeo. Roger.
Fucking prick.
Hotel two-six; this is Crazy Horse one-eight. Have individuals with weapons.
Yep, he's got a weapon, too.

Namir had over his shoulder his long lens camera, the one with optical zoom and was brilliant for getting long distance shots. One of the dozen men noticed it.

"What's its name?"

"What?"

"The camera; your camera? What's it called?"

Namir was slightly flummoxed by the question. "You know, it's not a pet," he cheerily informed the man.

"I know, but it looks so beautiful. People name their cars or ships after things, why not something so beautiful as that camera?"

Namir pondered this, but it was the younger Saeed who spoke, gently and sweetly.

"Namir hasn't yet realised how attached he is to his beautiful camera."

"Look, I know it has sentimental value, but it's not like a woman."

"Oh, but I heard you sleep with it."

"I have it close by."

"And you touch it at night."

"Stop being a pervert."

"Do you stroke it tenderly and caress it?"

"What, like you do your penis?"

The group of men laughed heartily, evidently enjoying the banter. They casually headed through the litter strewn, dusty streets and around the corner.

Hotel two-six, Crazy Horse one-eight. Have five to six individuals with AK47s. Request permission to engage.

Roger that. Uh, we have no personnel east of our position. So, uh, you are free to engage. Over.

All right, we'll be engaging.

Roger. Go ahead.

I'm gonna... I can't get them now because they're behind that building.

Um, hey Bushmaster element...

He's got an RPG!

Alright, we got a guy with a RPG.

I'm gonna fire.

The men stood by a wall while one eyed the helicopter.

"Hey, make sure you get a good photo of the helicopter when I hit it."

"*When*?" quipped another man. "Don't you mean if? You shoot like Wayne Rooney!"

"And what's wrong with Wayne Rooney? He's got a great shot."

"Fat and overrated, I'm afraid."

Saeed started laughing as Namir got his camera ready. Another of the men, more earnest in nature, derided the banter.

"What's wrong with you? This is about our freedom? We risk our lives for the future of our nation, so our children can be free; not because we can watch Wayne Rooney on the TV."

"You're right," added another man. "And anyway, I'd much rather watch Messi or Ronaldo."

"Bloody idiot! What are talking about?"

"Relax, I'm just making a joke of the situation."

The earnest man shook his head with some discern. "Joking? This is no time for jokes."

"Oh, but it's the perfect time," smile Namir. "How, in the insanity of war, can you pretend to be logical and rational?"

"Yes," agreed Saeed. "In such a mad situation it's better to be mad as well. War is mad – there's no point in making any sense of it."

The earnest man shook his head in disagreement. "So make jokes about Wayne Rooney and Lionel Messi."

"No, not Lionel Messi, just Wayne Rooney."

OK.

No, hold on. Let's come around. Behind buildings from our point of view.

Ok, we're gonna come around.

Hotel two-six; have eyes on individuals with RPG. Getting ready to fire. We won't...

Yeah, we had a guy shooting – and now he's behind the building.

God damn it.

Uh, negative. He was right in front of the Brad. Uh, about there, one o' clock. Haven't seen anything since then.

Just fuckin', once you get on 'em, just open 'em up.

Alright.

I see your element. Got about four Humvees, uh, out along. You're clear.

Alright, firing.

Let me know when you got them. Let's shoot. Light 'em all up.

Eight of the men stood together. Namir prepared to put his camera around his shoulder.

"Talking of fat people always makes me hungry," said Saeed with a degree of melancholy.

"Always thinking about food," grinned Namir as he swung his camera around his shoulder.

The earnest man was not amused.

"This is bloody serious, you bloody fools. What's wrong with you? Talking about eating and fat people and Wayne Rooney."

"Maybe we should eat," suggested Saeed.

"There's no time to eat, this is a war."

"Perfect time to eat," grinned Namir. "Don't worry, Saeed, we'll get some photos of this freedom fight and then we'll eat."

"Who'd be a journalist in a war?" sighed Saeed.

And that's when the shooting started.

Come on, fire
Keep shootin', 'n' keep shootin'. Keep shootin'. Keep shootin'
Hotel... Bushmaster Two-Six, Bushmaster Two-Six, we need to move time now.
Alright, we just engaged all eight individuals.
Yeah, we see two birds we're still firin'.

Namir ran but the gun was trained on him. He didn't stand a chance. Saeed also ran, but like his friend and colleague, Namir, he never stood a chance. The journalist and his assistance were killed almost instantly.

Got a bunch of bodies lying there.
Alright, we got about eight individuals.
Yeah, we got one guy crawling around down there, but, uh, you know, we got, definitely got something.
We're shooting some more.
Roger.
Hey, you shoot, I'll talk.

Oh yeah, look at those dead bastards.
Nice.
Good shootin'.
Thank you.

III

Masala turned around the corner into what could only be described as a scene befitting hell. Pools of dark red were forming in the parched earth; litter and debris were strewn everywhere as were corpses. The stench of death was fresh. Bodies sprawled around oozing blood, turning the dry dust a crimson red. Whatever had happened, had happened recently; the crimson dust had yet to settle.

Masala, Abdullah, Abdo and the two children stared in shock. Masala noticed one of the bodies was moving.

"Come on! Let's help him. We can take him to the hospital."

In a flash the three men jumped out the vehicle to help the wounded man.

Bushmaster; Crazy Horse. We have individuals going to the scene, looks like possibly, uh, picking up bodies and weapons. Let me engage. Roger. Break.

Uh, Crazy Horse One-Eight request permission to, uh, engage.

Picking up the wounded?

Yeah, we're trying to get permission to engage. Come on, let us shoot!

Bushmaster; Crazy Horse One-Eight.

In a panic and with racing hearts they managed to lift the dying man and get him into the rear of the vehicle. They eyed the helicopter above and knew they were in danger.

They're taking him.
Bushmaster; Crazy Horse One-Eight.

This is Bushmaster Seven, go ahead.
Roger. We have a black SUV, uh, Bongo truck picking up the bodies. Request permission to engage.
Fuck.
This is Bushmaster Seven, roger.
This is Bushmaster Seven, roger. Engage.
One-Eight, engage. Clear.
Come on!
Clear.
Clear.

As they got the wounded man into the van Masala began to pull off; the van didn't get very far, perhaps only a matter of yards, before being showered in a hail of bullets.

We're engaging.
Coming around. Clear. Roger. Trying to, uh,
Clear. I hear 'em co... I lost 'em in the dust. I got them.
I'm firing.
This is Bushmaster Forty, got any BDA on that truck? Over.
You're clear.
This is, uh, Crazy Horse. Stand By.
I can't shoot for some reason. I think the van's disabled.
Go ahead, shoot it.
I got an azimuth limit for some reason.
Go left.

Oh yeah, look at that. Right through the windshield!
Ha ha!

Eight minutes later ground troops arrived.

They just drove over a body.
Really?
Yeah.

The soldiers found two children in the van. The treating soldier decides to evacuate the children to the medical centre at the nearby base of Rustamiyah. However, higher command orders that the children are to be handed to Iraqi police and be taken to an Iraqi hospital instead.

Well, it's their fault for bringing their kids into a battle.
That's right.

St Petersburg, Russia.
October 1917

I

Vladimir burst excitedly through the door, almost yanking it off its rotten hinges.

"Anna! Anna!"

From behind the depleted shop counter a panic-stricken young lady emerged and proceeded to shove the young man out of the shop with great urgency.

"What are you doing coming here? Are you mad?"

"Anna, I must talk to you."

"You *must* leave."

"No, please, listen…"

"If father should come now…"

"Damn him and blast him!"

"Vladimir…"

"The Bolsheviks will deal with your father; he's a problem no more. That bourgeois pig…"

"I wish you wouldn't talk about him like that."

"Forget him for a moment, Joseph is outside standing guard, it's ok. Look, Anna, darling, please listen; there is something I must tell you."

The distressed young lady was clearly stricken by Vladimir's presence. He gently held her by both her arms and looked her directly in the eye.

"What is it? What's the matter? What's happened?"

"The Bolsheviks, in Moscow, they say they're going to bring the troops home from the war. It's incredible! They're rumours that Tsar Nicolas has been executed *and* the entire royal family. They're talking about giving land to the peasants… it's incredible… madness… the revolution has really happened Anna, Moscow is awash with red flags - red flags, Anna, with a hammer and I think a sickle …"

Vladimir yapped away excitedly about the revolution completely oblivious to Anna's discomfort. She fretted about not only her father returning unexpectedly to find her with her forbidden lover, but also the bad news she had yet to inform her lover of, and how indeed she was to inform him of such news.

The young revolutionary spoke as fast as sweat poured down his brow, even though it was a chilly, damp, St Petersburg evening. He huffed and puffed as he struggled to get his words out as quick as his mind would form them. The news of the past few months had been astonishing; the history of the last century more so. Serfs had achieved liberalisation and now had gone on to rule the landowners, the barons, the industrialists and the kings and queens, thanks to the Bolsheviks. A revolution truly had stirred. Not in Vladimir's wildest expectations did he have dream of such a scenario as this. His fervour and enthusiasm was not shared by Anna, however, as she had more pressing problems on her mind. Her indifference was a constant irritation to him.

"Father might…"

"Hang your father!"

"Vladimir! Don't talk like that."

"Damn him! The Bolsheviks will deal with that tyrant. He's an entrepreneur, a businessman, a capitalist, an exploiter, a profiteer of people's labour, a bastard! He's damned under the new system. Let's not waste our time worrying about the old guard."

The two fell silent whereby Vladimir gently placed his arms around Anna's slender frame and gently held her. He brushed her wispy, brown hair with his fingertips and kissed her forehead. She rested her head gently upon his chest so that she listened to his breathing and counted his heart beats for a moment –

all thoughts of her father momentarily and blissfully banished. She now pushed out of her mind the troubled secret she had yet to tell Vladimir and held him tightly in an all too short halcyon moment.

Again Vladimir held his trusted lover gently by her arms, locking his blue eyes onto her brown ones. "Oh, my precious lover, I must tell you something: Kolorav and Kasmarov are going to Moscow, and I'm to go with them…"

"*What*? What about me? What about *us*?"

"It's only for a month; two at the most. We need to see what's happening, what's going on. We're going to join the Bolsheviks; they need our help."

He waited for her to remonstrate, to protest, to say something, but instead she fell silent and turned away.

"You'll be fine for a month or two, won't you? Of course you will. I'll write to you, of course. You know I have so much to do and so much is going on. To think; no longer ruled by a tyrant monarchy but instead a president, a republic, a state for the workers. We'll smash the bourgeoisie and set up our utopia… what am I saying? They have been smashed! The capitalist, money-hungry, war pigs! And we are setting up our utopia, and I'm going to be part of it… part of history… Anna? Please, say something."

Anna surveyed the dirty-grey damp walls, the worn away rug beneath her feet, the stained windows of the shop front, the peeling yellow plaster from the ceiling. She caught a glimpse of herself in a cracked mirror and she saw her yellowing teeth, her sunken eyes and her thinning hair; her face was sallow and aged, like that of a woman who was worn from exhaustion. Illness, too, had taken its toll on her brittle frame, and she was not yet eighteen.

"Are you unwell? Is that it? The consumption that killed your mother…"

"I didn't bleed last month."

Vladimir waited for more but there was none.

"So? Why tell me? What do I care for such women's issue?"

"I've been sick the past two mornings."

"Do you want me to find a doctor for you? You know they are awfully expensive, especially at this time. Can your father not find a physician of sorts for you? I'm sure you'll be fine."

Anna took Vladimir's hand and put it upon her stomach. She looked into his blue eyes with intent then smiled while a tear rolled down her cheek. In absolute horror and totally aghast, Vladimir withdrew his hand, backing away as the realisation of what was happening hit him.

"We must get married, Vlad."

It was now his turn to avoid her eyes and dispassionately inspect the crumbling features of the store. His arched back now slouched as hers.

"Father will kill me. There is no doubt about that, he will kill me. He will kill you and he will kill me. He will kill us both. You must ask him for my hand, immediately, before I get big. I know he doesn't like you, but he'd accept you - he would!"

"He's never liked me!"

"He'd respect you for marrying me."

Vladimir surveyed the grim interior of the shop; it was all of a sudden a grim reflection of his life. He felt the nausea swell up inside him.

"Take me with you then. Take me with you to Moscow."

"Don't be ridiculous! We're revolutionaries signing up to aid the armed struggle; it's no place for a woman heavy with child."

"Then stay and marry me. What choice do we have? We have no money to elope with."

Vladimir turned his back on Anna and spoke with bitterness.

"I wanted to be a revolutionary; I wanted to help set up our workers' state. I thought perhaps one day I would study – for why should education be the preserve of the rich? I wanted to travel, to sample life, to taste adventure; to have my eyes opened and senses enriched." Opening his eyes wide and filing them with hate, he glared at his precious lover. "I wanted to live, and now I must put aside all dreams and provide for a child I that neither want nor cannot afford. Damn it! What place for love in a pragmatic world? What choice is there when there is no choice? Very well, I shall meet your brutish father and ask for your hand, then I shall inform my parents and we shall get married. Inform your father I will come to see him later this evening."

He sighed a despondent sigh, then, as if not to appear too defeated, he straightened his back, pushed back his shoulders, raised his head and lifted his eyebrows.

"The revolution will stop for no-one. I'll join the Bolsheviks here, in St Petersburg."

He left the shop without saying another word to his intended. Outside Joseph had been standing guard; Vladimir hastily grabbed his arm and made off into the dark, dreary streets of St Petersburg.

II

Karimov sat in the dimly lit room which occupied the space above his cloth shop. The candles burned steadily and mingled with the staleness. The windows could be opened to relieve the room of the stuffy and odious air that suffocated its inhabitants, but it was far too cold and therefore too dangerous to open them even a tad.

As Karimov sat pondering the more eventful events of his arduous day, in walked his only daughter, putting a smile on his worn, chubby and bearded face; his expression barely lasted a second as she was followed by that common, pig-farmer's son, Vladimir. He greeted Anna how he felt – with a smile, and also Vladimir - with a frown.

"Father, you look exhausted."

"That's because I am. Tell me, dear, what happened in the shop today? Did the Frenchman come?"

"He did, but he didn't want the cloth?"

"What?"

"He said times were too uncertain and until the restoration of order he feared for everything."

"Hang those blasted Mensheviks and Bolsheviks; as if things weren't bad enough already with the war."

"Father, they mean well. I hear Lenin is to bring the troops home. How torrid times have been; the poverty we have been subjected to; the hunger."

"Revolutionaries: heads full of dreams, brains full of shit."

Vladimir shifted uncomfortably in the background where shadows from the candles danced menacingly. Karimov noticed him, causing the young man to address his sweetheart.

"Can you wait outside for a moment, Anna? I need to talk to your father."

The young lady duly left, anxiously leaving lover and father to contest her future.

"Sir..."

"Please don't say you want to marry my daughter?"

"Sir, your daughter..."

"Oh, god, no; surely not..."

"Sir, I love..."

"What do you know of love? You - A tender eighteen year old."

"Sir, if only I could..."

"If only! If only! Life is full of ifs and buts!"

In an attempt to complete a sentence the young man raised his voice several octaves.

"Sir, I sincerely and with great fervour request that you would be kind enough to bequeath your daughter's hand to me."

The old man matched him by raising his deep, hoarse tones another notch.

"And why would I do such a thing? What can you offer her? What qualifications do you have? What of your education?"

"My education was cut short, Sir, as you well know. Academia was not affordable to my family. But I would like to study law very much, and the Bolsheviks say that education will be free for everyone and is not just the preserve of the rich."

"Bolshevik bullshit! What do they know? So what of your trade?"

"My father is a farmer, Sir."

"What kind of farmer?"

"You know, Sir."

"What kind? Let me hear you say it, boy."

"He's a... pig farmer."

"Sorry, I didn't quite catch that."

Karimov cupped his ear.

"A... *pig* farmer."

"*Swine*? Mmmm, that's delicious. Now tell me young man, what funds do you have? Investments? Properties?"

"You know, Sir, I have none."

"I see. So tell me, why the hell would I bequeath my daughter to a man with no education, a man whose trade is to bathe pigs and clean their shit, and a man of no means and whose only inheritance is a filthy pig-farm?"

"Because, Sir, I love your daughter."

"Liar! I've seen you. As far as I can see she's never been good enough for you, and now you want to marry her. Why don't you tell me why you really want to marry her?"

"I've already told you..."

"A depraved liar!"

The speed and efficiency at which Karimov dispatched his words left Vladimir trailing behind. The young man had no choice other than to allow the businessman to have his rant before acting.

"I would rather have my penis sliced with a sickle than have my only daughter be wed to you, for what right thinking man would agree to such an arrangement? How will you support her when you have no money and no means of making any? What kind of life would she have as the wife of a pig-farmer? My aim in life, or at least one of my aims, is to better myself from whence I came, and for my children, of which there now only remains dear Anna, to be better than me. So tell me, young, naïve, ignorant, uneducated, poor, pig-farmer, tell me, how can I marry my daughter to you when she happens to be the daughter of a successful businessman, an entrepreneur who was making thousands of roubles each year before this damned war started? *Her* father is a man of means and standing, whereas *your* father, if you have one…"

Karimov stopped to look at the oaf who was contesting to be his son-in-law; he was matched with a hard stare from the young man who had inched closer.

"What's this? Praise the Lord! The boy has turned into a man. Are you going to strike me? Hang you and curse you!"

"So, you won't give us your blessing?"

"Didn't you hear anything I said? Kill me before I accept such an ungainly union, which I suspect you might. What's that? A pistol you carry?"

"In these troubled times I can help you, but you don't want my help do you, you fat, pig-headed bastard!"

Karimov, shocked by this brazen attitude, leant forward in his rotting chair before attempting to stand, only to be unceremoniously pushed back down.

"Such insolence!" he cried. "Arrogance and ignorance: two ingredients of youth, of which you have both in abundance."

"Shut your wretched hole, old man; your time is up, your chance is gone."

Karimov sat motionless, unable to believe the peasant's front.

"Shoot me, then. Go on, bloody peasant, shoot me!"

Vladimir went to the door and called out. A moment later, Leon and joseph appeared followed by a frantic Anna.

"Vladimir? What's happening? Father? Vladimir? Please explain what is happening."

"Quiet!" screamed Vladimir at the woman he planned to marry. He addressed his two colleagues. "This man is an enemy of the revolution. He is a capitalist, shamelessly exploiting the labour of the people manufacturing his cloths. He despises peasants, the poor, the workers, the ones who give their blood and sweat for this country. He is a disgrace who deals in free trade! Take him away! Let the courts decide what to do with such a bourgeois pig. Take him and hand him to the Bolsheviks!"

"You ruffian! You peasant! How dare you seize me! You'll never get away with this!"

"Go on, get out! This store now belongs to the people of Russia! We'll create a union in this store, a soviet. No more exploitation of the workers!"

"Damn you! I've worked hard my whole life! Everything I have I worked day and night for. Hang you!"

Despite his protestations the capitalist was overpowered by the young revolutionaries. Anna, horrified by the on-goings, turned to her lover in desperation.

"What are you doing? Vladimir, this is my father. You can't do this, not to my father. Vlad, if you loved me, you wouldn't do this."

Vladimir ignored her, instead needlessly giving Karimov a couple of kicks as he was eventually dragged from the room.

"Vladimir, please… My father slaves day and night; he's just a small shopkeeper…"

"For crying out loud woman, have I not enough to attend to without your whining?"

"You can't have my father arrested."

"Can and have."

"Please, Vladimir, he's my father and he's hardly one of those rich upper class industrialists…"

"He's an enemy…"

"Then so am I."

"Don't be stupid."

"It's true; I'm sick of all this… this revolution nonsense; I hate it. It's stupid. I want to be with my father. We're not rich. Look around you: the wall paper is peeling, our windows are cracked, the floorboards are rotten. All my life my father and I have struggled. If he's an enemy then so am I."

Vladimir fell silent and addressed Anna earnestly. "Very well, then." He went to the window and saw Karimov being bundled into a horse and cart. Joseph was standing guard outside, as usual. Vladimir beckoned him into the store.

"Joseph, take her away."

"Where to?"

"To be questioned. She professes to be an enemy of the revolution."

"Go on then, you bastard," goaded Anna. "Send me and your unborn to Siberia."

"I will; where you all will be better off and out the way. Joseph, seize her!"

Joseph stood statuesque like.

"I can't," he quietly said.

"What? I command you!"

"We're of equal rank," coldly said Joseph, fingering his moustache.

"What's wrong with you? She confesses to be an enemy; she is the daughter of a bourgeois pig who exploits and abuses the poor."

Joseph drew a pistol from beneath his tatty shirt, which was a lot filthier than Vladimir's, and took aim.

"Sorry," whispered the gunman. "But I think I should be the one giving the orders. It's for the best."

"What..? Why...? How..?" stuttered an astonished Vlad, whose blood withdrew from his face and left him as pale as death.

"Because… I love her."

As one young revolutionary tried to make sense of the other's actions and words, a bullet entered his head from one side and left from the other, taking with it fragments of tissue and cells alike, and rendering the young man dead. As his body lay motionless with blood oozing from his wound, the two remaining characters watched with a morbid curiosity.

"It's ok," said Joseph after a while, placing his arms around Anna and turning her head from the sight of the corpse. "I'll take care of you, my sweet."

"And what about father?"

"Let him go. It is better he is out of the way."

Anna placed her troubled, young and exhausted head on Joseph's chest. She closed her sunken eyes as he tenderly squeezed her; she didn't reciprocate.

Birkenhau-Auschwitz, Poland.
January 1943

I

General Von Schmitten's large feet were well insulated against the thick winter snow; this pleased him considerably. Not only did his socks come from the woolliest sheep in Scandinavia, but his boots appeared to be made from the finest cows that the Reich possessed. Good, purely bred, Nazi cows, who would produce the finest and sternest leather, thought Von Schmitten. His mind turned towards that evening's dinner and the steak he could look forward to devouring. He mused over the sauce and the wine that would be served with it and whether any cheese and bread rolls would come as he'd requested.

"General! General!"

Von Schmitten turned to find one of the Privates hurdling his way through the snow. "Damn it," he muttered to himself, aggrieved that his only moment of solitude that day had been abruptly interrupted. "Is there never a moment's peace to be had during this war?"

"General! General!"

The sky was a dirty white with heavy clouds lingering; at the horizon it blended neatly with the dirty white of the snow; snow that was now several feet tall. The General cautiously stepped over it and into it, leaving behind polar bear like prints in the arctic. Indeed, the arctic is what it felt like, and Von Schmitten couldn't help but momentarily fantasise about being one of those explorers on a daring expedition to get to the centre of the North Pole. He yearned for that sense adventure: the thrills and the rewards, the challenges and the education, the stories he could tell his children and the rare, precious gifts he would bring back for his wife. Yes, to be an explorer was so much better than being a General in the Reich and being stuck in this hell of a place.

"General!"

"What? What is it?"

The Private saluted his superior.

"Sir, you have a telegram, Sir."

"Well, where is it?"

"Sir, I don't know, Sir."

"Well, what fucking good is that? Is it here or at Auschwitz?"

"Sir, I don't know, Sir. General Von Blinken only informed me to pass this message to you. That's all I know, Sir."

"You don't know much, do you?"

"Sir, no, Sir."

The two men stood entrenched in the snow and from a distance they appeared to be smoking, such was the mist coming from their mouth.

"*Well?*" snapped Von Schmitten so harshly and unexpectedly that the Private almost jumped out of his skin.

"Sir?"

"Well? What now?"

The Private shifted his feet uncomfortably in the snow, more at unease with his superior rather than the cumbersome weather conditions. His nervousness became clearly reflected in his speech, which, like a cycle of sorts, only served his anxiety.

"Erm... Nothing, Sir... That's it, Sir... I was only to deliver the... erm... message..."

"Really?" mocked Von Schmitten.

"Sir, yes, Sir. I am to report back to General Von Blinken... Sir."

"Well, what are you waiting for? Go on, then. *Fuck off*!"

114

The Private saluted and was thankful to make his way back to Von Blinken. Von Schmitten sighed, releasing a pool of mist into the crisp mid-day winter air, and made his way back to the main reception where he hoped the telegram would be. As he trampled the snow he gave thanks for his heavy coat and gloves.

Birkenhau was the size of several football pitches and dotted by various wooden huts where prisoners would live. To avoid these, largely because of the disease to be found there, Von Schmitten walked parallel to one of the many eight foot tall wire fences which surrounded the perimeter and was decorated with cold barb-wire. Whilst doing so, his mind again retuned to the thought of that evening's dinner. Yesterday's had been a real disappointment; the potatoes had been cooked for way too long, and the chicken was far too tender. He looked forward to venison again; it felt a while since he had had that. But what he really yearned for wasn't a supremely well-cooked main, or a delightful starter, but a good dessert; a piece of finely baked cake would go down very well, thought Von Schmitten as he reached the main reception.

He gave his name to the receptionist who then went scampering off to retrieve the telegram. Such was her ugliness that Von Schmitten suspected her of being a Jew; certainly, her genetic background needed to be investigated as it must surely be a crime to have conceived such a beast.

She returned and wearily handed the telegram to Von-Schmitten. 'God, you really are ugly,' thought the General as he tried to supress the regurgitation of his lunch of cold sausage and finely roasted vegetables. Then again, perhaps her shocking features might actually be improved by having a hail of vomit spewed onto them. Von Schmitten grinned as he took the telegram without saying a word.

II

Major Fekumard was a busy man. A million things needed to be done and the days never allowed for enough hours for them to be accomplished. Accomplished, however, is exactly what Fekumard was, having all sorts of medals attached to his chest. Indeed, he was a relic of the old Weimar days and one that well remembered Germany's inglorious surrender in 1918. Over zealousness characterised his career whence he would take orders as far as he could, thriving upon the extreme nature of politics.

He sat at his desk: signing papers, reading papers, writing papers, shuffling papers. He didn't look up at Von Schmitten.

"How are you General?"

"I'm very well, thank you, Major."

"Good, good. Well, straight to the point, what is it? I gather that if you're here then it's not for the purpose of a social visit."

"It's my wife, Major. She's… we've, had a boy."

Von Schmitten paused, waiting for a response, but Fekumard merely remained preoccupied with his papers.

"Congratulations," he said after a while, without feeling.

"Thank you, Major."

The General was hesitant and felt and looked awkward. He thought hard about how best to phrase his request.

"Is there more, General? Do you wish me to be a god-parent? Huh?"

"No, Major. I just wondered, or hoped, rather, whether I could be granted leave, just for a few days, to see my wife and my new born son?"

"I will put in the request but you have no chance of it being granted. We're in a war you know."

"I know, Sir. It's just that it's been so long since I've seen my wife…"

"Well, you must have seen her about nine months ago."

"Yes, Major. It's just that my youngest is sick. I already have two children, and I miss them so dearly, surely a few days leave can be arranged, for what harm can it do? I come from a small family; my wife doesn't have many people around her. Her well-being is of a grave concern to me…"

Fekumard finally looked up at his colleague with exasperation; he removed his spectacles from his chubby face and placed them upon his greasy head. He spoke with little patience.

"We're in the midst of a war, General. Each day is as critical, if not more so, than the last. We all make sacrifices. Don't you think I'd like nothing more than to be at home in the warm comfort of my family's bosom? Which one of these men wouldn't right now pass up the opportunity to be with their wives or children? You are over-come by emotion right now; is your son healthy?"

"As far as I know, Major."

"Then be grateful for that. We shall toast him this evening."

He dropped his glasses back onto his face, taking with them the grease they had collected from his hair. His papers regained their importance as again he gave them his undivided attention.

"Is there anything more, General?"

Von Schmitten thought about asking what sauce would be served with the beef tonight, and whether the bread rolls and wine would come with the cheese, but he thought better of it.

"Erm… No, Major. Thank you. Heil Hitler."

"Heil Hitler."

As Von Schmitten turned to go back out into the arctic conditions, his superior gave him a final piece of advice.

"Remember, General, you are here fighting for the future of your children – be consoled with that."

III

War has no knowledge of days or months or years; time is a luxury afforded to peace. Yesterday would be the same as today as it would be tomorrow. War knows nothing of calendars, of families, of husbands and wives and of sons or daughters. Today was Sunday, but it could well have been any day.

Von Schmitten sighed. It was another two hours before the next train of arrivals, until then he resolved to walk by himself around the perimeter of the camp; there he could be alone with his thoughts, keeping only the barbed-wire fence and the occasional watchtower for company. His thoughts, however, would not stray further than his family. His son: what did he look like? His dear wife: How was her health? How was she coping? His two other daughters, how were they? How their hair must have grown as their bodies. What were they all doing? Were they really ok, in this mess of a war?

As he grappled with the uncertainty he noticed a group of prisoners digging a rather large hole in the ground.

"You need it a bit deeper," shouted Von Schmitten to a Private supervising the prisoners. "Otherwise the bodies will putrefy."

"No, Sir, it's the foundations for another chamber, Sir."

"Oh, I see."

How to escape this madness and get back to Berlin, just for a few days? As he battled with his turmoil he strolled past a solitary prisoner digging what looked to be his own grave. Such was the General's need for conversation at that moment he suddenly took leave of his surroundings and addressed the stick-like prisoner.

"Today should be the happiest and proudest day of my life: my wife gave birth to my son." Von Schmitten didn't look at the prisoner; instead he eyed a solitary crow flying by. "I should be with my dear wife, my children, my parents, my long-suffering family. Instead, I am here."

As if to emphasise the fact, Von Schmitten turned around with his hands out. "Here: in this shithole, doing all this shit, because it's so much more important than anything else. Do they think the war effort will cease if I go home for two days? Will the Soviets over run us in the east? Will the Americans suddenly invade the south? Will the British launch an invasion from the west? What nonsense! My absence would cause no more of an inconvenience than one of the Fuhrer's afternoon naps."

"I had a family," the prisoner muttered in a barely audible whisper without ceasing his digging.

Von Schmitten now noticed him. "Children?"

The man stopped to remember. "A girl and a boy. They were beautiful children, beautiful. I came here seven months ago with them and my parents. I haven't seen any of them since. I don't know anything."

Von Schmitten looked at the skeletal figure in his filth-ridden, striped uniform. 'Indeed', he thought to himself, 'my problems really aren't so severe.'

"Can you find out for me what happened to them? I am to be shot tomorrow morning. I would die more peacefully if I knew they were ok. Then again, which of us is really ok in this place?"

Von Schmitten looked away. "You know I cannot do that."

He expected the prisoner to remonstrate but instead the man continued digging his own grave.

"Why are you to be shot?"

"I helped two Polish prisoners escape. They had good knowledge of the local area, and like everyone else here, they were going mad. They wanted to find out what had become of their wives and children, their fathers and mothers."

"I heard about that. It was all of two weeks ago. Why are they executing you now?"

"I have been in Block Eleven since then, in solitary confinement."

Again Von Schmitten turned his thoughts to his own wife and children, to his parents; he became subdued as melancholy weighed him down.

"You know, I often feel like making a run for it myself."

Ceasing his digging, the prisoner looked up with hope. "Well, why don't you? We could make a plan. We could both break out. I'm sure with you being a General it would be easy. I know the routine of the guards at the back and I know…"

Von Schmitten shook his head. "No, they would find us. It would be impossible to escape, then we'd both be shot."

The prisoner continued with his digging.

"I am sorry I cannot help you." Von Schmitten turned to walk away with a burrowed brow, but paused. "Look, I can't help you in that way, but I can save your life. I can have an amnesty granted for you. You shan't be killed."

Panting heavily, the prisoner suddenly became galvanized, showing more zest than he had done since his incarceration at the camp. He dropped his tool and looked up in disbelief at the troubled General.

"No! Please! Please, let me die! I can't take any more of this! I want to die! You must let me die! It's hell – *hell,* I tell you! I've only eaten stale bread for as far back as I can remember. I sleep in a hut with a hundred men - it's ridden with disease. There are six men alone on my bunk. There are no mattresses and the conditions are freezing and…" The prisoner wailed hysterically as Von Schmitten struggled for words. "No! Please! Don't let me live! Please! Not here! I can't take it anymore! I can't go on! You've got to kill me! This is hell! Don't you understand? This is hell on earth! Please! I've lost everything and everyone! All my family…"

In a throw of desperation the prisoner stumbled out of his half-dug grave and threw himself at the General's feet. "You *must* let me die! You *must*! You *must*! Save someone else…Please! Please! I can't live like this anymore, like *animals*!"

The sight of a prisoner clutching his feet only served to draw attention to himself. Almost inevitably a Private came running over.

"Everything alright, General?" The Private drew his pistol. "Shall I shoot him?"

"Yes! Yes! Shoot me! Please! Please!" Tears streaked down his cheeks as he turned to Von Schmitten. "If you had any decency about you, you would end my suffering. You wouldn't let an animal suffer this much."

Completely unsure of what to do or how to act, the General ordered the Private to take the prisoner back to his hut. As the Private neared the prisoner grew more hysterical, clutching Von Schmitten's finely crafted and well insulated leather boots ever tighter.

"Look, I am trying to help you."

The Private approached and the prisoner took flight.

"Look, I'm escaping! You must shoot me! I'm going to escape! You have to shoot me now!" He threw himself onto the barbed-wire only for the Private to haul him off.

The prisoner was dragged away past a gas chamber, wailing and pleading to be put out of his miserable existence, leaving behind a trail of blood on the virgin white snow from where the barbed-wire had torn his fragile, emaciated skin.

General Von Schmitten wasn't quite sure whether what he had witnessed was sanity or not – possibly half-way between, he mused. It had become hard to differentiate between the two, and often under war, there is no difference. What is madness in peacetime is normality in war; what is wrong is right, and then later it becomes wrong again. Our morals and beliefs are turned upside down and inside out.

He observed one of the gas chambers being constructed in front of him, and then thought about his family before once again returning his thoughts to that evening's dinner; how he hoped the cheese and bread rolls would be served tonight. He thought about all the killing and dying he had seen and how much of it was necessary to achieve Lebensraum. Hadn't that been accomplished? How much living space did the Fuhrer want? Belguim, Holland, half of France, half of Poland and half of Scandinavia had all been conquered. And what did the Jews really have to do with it all? In the end it was all too much for his mind to bear so instead he walked around the camp, imagining himself to be in the Arctic on a wild expedition, looking out for penguins and polar bears. There in the North Pole, there was no war, no concentration camps, and no wives giving births to sons; no people begging to die. So it is there he remained for his Sunday afternoon stroll.

Amiens, France.
August 8th 1918

In the early hours of a damp August morning, German military forces strolled through Luxembourg before going on to rape Belgium. A battle then ensued with French forces, aided by some Brits, whereby after some to-ing and fro-ing the two sides dug themselves in along a line stretching from the North Sea to the Franco-Swiss border. This line, largely unchanged for most of the war, came to be known as the Western Front.

At 4am on 8th August 1918, along the Front in Northern France, just north of the bloodied River Somme and not far from the devastated and occupied town of Amiens, there was stationed a British Military Force, whose infantry soldiers stood in complete silence in their rancid trenches. Encompassed by darkness and total silence, they prepared to go over the top; to go across the 500 yards of no-man's land that had separated them from both their German cousins and foes, in a battle that would begin the end of this most brutal and futile of wars.

As the dense fog drifted into the putrid trenches, worn British soldiers, hungry, exhausted, sick, and in many cases traumatised, stood anxiously awaiting a signal to begin the charging; each man alone with his thoughts.

Two friends and colleagues stood side by side, one taking deep breaths, the other anxiously fingering the butt of his rifle. Private Walker: thin, sallow face; dirty uniform, filthy and just generally covered in shit, quietly whispered to Private Headman, who was not of an altogether different disposition, being that he, too,

*was of poor physical health and of equally poor attire,
being that he, too, appeared to be covered in shit.*

WALKER
Eddie, what the fuck's goin' on?

HEADMAN
We're goin' over the top.

WALKER
You what?

HEADMAN
We're goin' over the bleedin' top.

WALKER
What top?

HEADMAN
You know, out there. We're going out there to fight.

WALKER
Out there? You're fuckin' jokin' aintchya? There's a
load o' Germans up there.

HEADMAN
The skipper's been given the orders. We're goin' over
the top to fight Jerry.

Brief pause

WALKER
I'm not.

HEADMAN
What?

130

WALKER
I ain't goin' up there, I'll get killed.

HEADMAN
What? You scared or somethin'?

WALKER
Fuckin' terrified! Can't you smell me trousers?

Private Headman sniffs the air around Walker's arse

HEADMAN
You really are shitting it, mate. Well, you gotta, fight, or else it's the firing squad for you. At least you got a chance of survivin' with Jerry out 'ere. I mean, you've got your pistol and stick to face all those machine guns 'n' artillery shells 'ere, but at the range you ain't got nuthin'; they blindfold you, tie you to a tree 'n'..."

WALKER
Why are we fightin'?

HEADMAN
You what?

WALKER
What we fightin' for?

HEADMAN
You ask some daft questions. 'Ow the fuck do I know? Some Austrian bloke got killed somewhere in Serbia, or something.

WALKER

So what are we doin' 'ere, in France, fightin' the Germans?

HEADMAN
I ain't sure. Could be something to do with Belgium?

WALKER
Belgium? What's Belgium got to do with anything?

HEADMAN
Dunno. But they reckon they make some fine chocolate there. And beer. Not like the crap we get back 'ome.

WALKER
Did the Austrian bloke want some chocolate or beer or something?

HEADMAN
Dunno. I think the Russians got a lot o' the chocolate 'n' it pissed off Jerry, or somethin'. It can't be the beer 'cos they've got a load of vodka there.

WALKER
Well, it ain't nothin' to do with me, all this killing business. I got wife 'n' kids back in Peck'am, I ain't got time for any of this malarkey. I'm off.

From behind and above the trench appears Captain Greylord. He, too, is of slim build, but unlike the other two his uniform is spotless and he does not stink of shit. He is a positively dull man, and not the brightest, reliant as he was, and still is, on those old school tie networks. He keeps his voice low to maintain the necessary silence.

GREYLORD

I say, what's going on down there? What's all the kerfuffle about?

HEADMAN
It's Private Walker, Sir. 'E's scared.

GREYLORD
Scared?

WALKER
Yes, Sir. I'm fuckin' terrified, I am.

GREYLORD
Terrified?

WALKER
Yes, Sir; terrified of dying, Sir. I don't wanna die.

GREYLORD
I see.
(He mulls this over.)
Oh, go on, be a sport.

WALKER
No chance, Sir. I'd rather face the firing squad.

GREYLORD
That's a shame. And a bit of an inconvenience; we're, I mean, *you're*, about to go over the top, you know. Mmmm...
(He again pauses for thought)
Private Walker, tell me, with firing squad it's certain death, up in no man's land, you have a chance. So if you're afraid of dying, surely you should take your chance up there.

HEADMAN
'At's what I said to him, Sir.

WALKER
There could be monsters up there.

HEADMAN *(laughing)*
What? Like Big Foot?

GREYLORD
I can assure you, my good man, there are no monsters up there, just bombs and bullets and things. Monsters do not even exist.

WALKER
They do, Sir. When I go to sleep I see 'em. They haunt me they do.

GREYLORD
My good man, that happens to be what we call: a *dream*.

HEADMAN
Or in his case, Sir, a *nightmare*

GREYLORD *(laughing)*
Yes, yes, very good Private Headman, very good.

WALKER
Well, I been gassed, I been shot at, I 'ad artillery shells 'n' grenades go off in me face, I 'ad bombs dropped on me; 'alf me mates are dead, 'n' I dunno where the other 'alf are. 'At's not a dream, is it?

HEADMAN *(laughing with Captain Greylord)*

Sounds like another nightmare to me. You really need to get out more.

GREYLORD
Yes, lighten up Private Headman. Drink some fine wine and relax until your heart is content. Once the war is over, I mean.

WALKER
The monsters…

GREYLORD
For King George's bottom's sake, there are no monsters. Only bullets and bombs, bits of shrapnel and things like that.

Field Marshall Hagery-Grave comes over to see what all the noise is about. He is a butch man, broad chest and shoulders, and without doubt, well-fed. He sports a broad handlebar moustache, and has towering eyebrows just as well-groomed. His uniform is impressive with all the stripes and medals attached to it. To keep himself warm, he adorns a large overcoat. Field Marshal Hagery-Grave has the unfortunate affliction of being unable to speak in a whisper, rather he roars his way through life.

HAGERY-GRAVE *(angry)*
I say, what the Jolly farmer's is going on down there? You're supposed to be in silence, preparing for the *big push*.

GREYLORD
It's Private Walker, Field Marshall, he don't wanna fight.

HAGERY-GRAVE
And why is that? Scared is he?

HEADMAN
Yes, Sir, 'e's scared like a little girl.

WALKER
I'm shitting it, M' Lord.

HAGERY-GRAVE
M' Lord? I'm a Field Marshall not a Lord, well not yet.
Now then, you bumbling imbecile, what's all this
nonsense about *being scared*?

WALKER
I'm shitting bricks, Master. My trousers are covered in
me own filth.

HEADMAN
It's true, Sir. I sniffed 'em, I did.

GREYLORD
Yes, it's true Field Marshall, I can smell them from
here.

HEADMAN
Sounds like you've already discharged yourself from
the army!

GREYLORD (*laughing*)
I say, Private Headman, you do exceed yourself. Ever
thought about a career in stand-up?

HAGERY-GRAVE
Shut up, you moronic buffoons! Now then, I've yet to
hear something so damned ridiculous as: *being scared*.

What is this foreign concept? Well, it must be foreign, because *being scared* isn't a British trait now, is it?

WALKER
I don't wanna die, Your Majesty.

HAGERY-GRAVE
Idiot! If we weren't surrounded by all the other soldiers I'd shoot you myself, right here. One doesn't know how lucky one is. If only I could be in your place: being in the heart of battle, being shot at, bayonetted and gassed, trying to avoid being blown to smithereens. Oh, how lucky you are! I have the misfortune of conducting everything from the safety of the side-lines.

WALKER
I'd rather face the firing squad, Your Holiness.

HAGERY-GRAVE
Moronic rectum slurper! You'd have more chance of surviving up there in no-man's land than you would facing the firing squad, bloody idiot!

GREYLORD
That's what I told him, Field Marshall.

HEADMAN
Me 'n' all. But 'e's a bum-lover, Sir.

HAGERY-GRAVE *(eyes light up)*
A sodomist, hey. Really?

HEADMAN
Erm... No, Sir. 'E's got wife 'n' kids. I don't really mean what I say, ain't 'at right?

HAGERY-GRAVE
Are you speaking foreign?

GREYLORD
He means that he is speaking metaphorically, Field
Marshall.

HEADMAN
Erm… If you say so, Sir.

HAGERY-GRAVE *(addresses Private Headman)*
So what about you, my good man?

HEADMAN
No, Sir. I ain't never buggered no-one in me life.

HAGERY-GRAVE
Fool! I'm not asking you about your sexual
preferences, I mean are you a scaredy puss-puss like
Private Walker over here? Are you, too, the poo-in-
your-pants kind?

HEADMAN
No, Sir. I'm nothin' like Private Headman.

HAGERY-GRAVE
Good man!

HEADMAN
But I don't wanna fight either, Sir.

HAGERY-GRAVE
What? Why the devil not?

HEADMAN
Well, I dunno what I'm fighting for, Sir.

HAGERY-GRAVE
What kind of base moron are you?

HEADMAN
A confused one, Sir.

HAGERY-GRAVE
Tell him why we're fighting, Captain Greylord.

GREYLORD
Well, as far as I can make out, because the Germans
invaded Belgium, and by the treaty of London, signed
in 1839, where we guaranteed to protect Belgium's
independence....

HAGERY-GRAVE *(face red with anger)*
Bloody arsehole! Am I surrounded by pig-loving
jesters? Am I the only sane person in this war?
Belgium? Belgium? What's *Belgium* got to do with
anything?

HEADMAN
They make some fine chocolate there, I 'eard.

WALKER
And beer, not like the crap we get back 'ome.

HAGERY-GRAVE
Listen, you dense, poorly-bred ignoramuses; we are
here fighting Jerry because if we don't stop him he'll
take over the world. Can you imagine that, the Germans
running the world and sticking their noses in
everyone's affairs?

GREYLORD

Surely that's our job, Field Marshall?

HAGERY-GRAVE
Precisely, Captain Greylord. Can you imagine a world where you would have to eat German sausage and drink German beer?

WALKER
I got wife 'n' kids back 'ome to think of.

HAGERY-GRAVE
Haven't we all?

HEADMAN
I 'avne't, Sir.

HAGERY-GRAVE *(rubbing his hands excitedly)*
Do you have more of a predilection towards those of a more masculine nature?

HEADMAN
What?

HAGERY-GRAVE
Do you like men's bottoms?

HEADMAN
I certainly do not, Sir. I got a girlfriend, she's me fiancé.

HAGERY-GRAVE
And I guess you, like every other bumbling idiot, would rather be in the safety of your lover's arms?

HEADMAN

No chance, Sir. She's evil. 'Er name's Anne Diamond, she's a thieving little whore. She's just been made 'ead of the Forty Elephants. They're a gang, they are. I'm fuckin' terrified of 'em.

GREYLORD
Well if you're terrified of her, don't marry her then. Simple.

HEADMAN
But it ain't that simple, Captain.

GREYLORD
Why not?

HEADMAN
'Cos im fuckin' terrified of 'er.

HAGERY-GRAVE
That's precisely the point you dithering idiot; if you're frightened of her, then don't marry her.

HEADMAN
But if I don't marry 'er, she'll kill me.

HAGERY-GRAVE
I'd kill you myself if we weren't surrounded by the other soldiers.

WALKER
You'll probably get killed up there with all the monsters anyway.

HAGERY-GRAVE
Monsters? Are you a dithering imbecile? A moron?

WALKER
Yes, Oh Great One. Can I go 'ome now?

HAGERY-GRAVE
Has one not heard of the Hapsburg Empire? Austro-Hungary?

WALKER
I'm starving, Master.

HEADMAN
Me 'n' all. The rations are like vomit and faeces mashed together, and we're better off drinking our own urine.

HAGERY-GRAVE
Senseless bastards! I'm talking about *Hungary*, not *hungry*!

WALKER
Yeah, I'm famished.

HEADMAN
I could eat an 'orse.

GREYLORD
He means the *country* Hungary.

WALKER
Which country's hungry?

HEADMAN
It can't be Russia 'cos they got all the chocolate, didn't they, Sir?

HAGERY-GRAVE

Foolish swines! Don't you know anything? Have you never heard of Austria-Hungary? The Hapsburg Empire?

HEADMAN
So Austria's 'ungry; is that why they're fighting the Germans, cos Jerry got all the chocolate?

HAGERY-GRAVE (Indignant)
Blasted imbeciles! Austria and Germany are allies! We're fighting against those devilish countries!

WALKER
I thought we was fightin' the French, Master.

HAGERY-GRAVE
The French are our allies you... Are you the son of a woman whose business it is to fornicate with strangers and perform lewd acts both on them and for them in order to receive monetary gain?

WALKER
Yes. Can I leave now, Your Majesty?

HAGERY-GRAVE
You certainly may not. Now then, I'm talking about history you bastards. You see, Serbia, which is where the heir to the Austrian throne, Archduke Ferdinand, was killed by a Serbian nut; Serbia was formerly the territory of the Ottoman Empire. As the Turks are rapidly losing their power a kind of power vacuum exists over the region where the Austrians and Germans have their greedy eyes upon Serbia and dare I say the entire Balkan region. But remember, the Serbians are jolly good chums with their fellow Slavs the Russians. As for Turkey...

WALKER
Oh, yes please! I can't remember the last time I 'ad turkey.

HEADMAN
Me 'n' all! I'll 'ave a bit. I ain't never 'ad no turkey, none, never.

WALKER
Me neither. I ain't never 'ad no turkey, none, never either neither.

HAGERY-GRAVE (to Captain Greylord)
Why are they speaking in tongue, Captain Greylord?

GREYLORD
It's just their way of expressing themselves, Field marshal.

HEADMAN
At Christmas me 'n' me family all look at a picture of a turkey.

WALKER
You got a picture? You lucky sod! We just go to the rich people's area and smell the turkeys cooking. We close our eyes 'n' pretend we're eating it.

HAGERY-GRAVE
Thick vagrants! Has one never heard of the Ottoman Empire? Turkey? Not the bird! The blasted country!

WALKER
I don't understand, Your Majesty.

HEADMAN
Me neither.

HAGERY-GRAVE
I'm exasperated, Captain Greylord! I'm positively flabbergasted. Is such the baseness of our soldier's intellect that they neither understand that Hungry and Turkey are countries?

WALKER
Is the turkey hungry, Master?

HEADMAN
If the turkey were 'ungry they'd feed it, so it can't be 'ungry.

WALKER
They might've run out of turkey food.

HEADMAN
There ain't no such thing as turkey food. What they eat is grass.

WALKER
They don't eat grass.

HEADMAN
'Course they do. They're like cows 'n' sheep.

WALKER
No they ain't.

HEADMAN
Well, they eat grass anyway, ain't that so Captain Greylord 'n' Field Marshall. Turkey's eat grass, don't they?

HAGERY-GRAVE
Be quiet you pair of wankers! Now then, Captain Greylord, it's obvious what's wrong with these men.

GREYLORD
And what's that Field Marshall?

HAGERY-GRAVE
Well, the reason they are scared and confused is because they don't have their Captain with them in battle.

WALKER
No, Oh Great One. The reason I don't wanna fight is 'cos I'm scared the monsters are gonna eat me.

HEADMAN
And the reason I don't wanna fight is 'cos I can't make 'ead nor tail of nufink. I mean, the Germans are tryin' to take over the world, like what we done with our Empire, but there's some Serbian bloke in Austria who got shot, and he's hungry and don't like Russia 'cos the Russians ate all the chocolate, bastards, from Belguim. And 'cos of the treaty in 1329 we 'ave to attack France. And no one's feedin' the turkeys. I don't understand nuffink.

HAGERY-GRAVE
Well, if you do not understand nothing, you must understand everything. Splendid! All is well! Captain Greylord, you will accompany your men in battle.

GREYLORD
What? But Field Marshall…

146

HAGERY-GRAVE
I know Captain; no need to thank me.

GREYLORD
But I have a wife, Field Marshall. And we plan to have a family - a big family; three or four children, and maybe some pets, like a small dog...

HAGERY-GRAVE
And think about the tales you can tell them about how you dodged all those bullets and shells and survived those gas attacks, you plucky, lucky man.

GREYLORD
But, Field Marshall, please...

HAGERY-GRAVE
Express your thanks another time, Captain. There's no time now.
(Pushes Captain Greylord into the trench)
Well, tally-ho then. And hoorah to giving Jerry a big kick up his elementary canal!

Hagery-Grave departs, leaving the trio in the trench braced for the signal to go over the top. The lights in the trench go out.

WALKER
What do we do now?

HEADMAN
Brace yourself. You alright Captain? You look a bit pale.

GREYLORD
Yes, yes. I don't feel well. I think we're all about to
die. Are we?

HEADMAN (*smiling*)
Yes, we are, Captain. We're all about to be blown to
smithereens!

GREYLORD
You sound awfully exuberant.

HEADMAN
Ex-cuber-what?

GREYLOD
Happy. You sound awfully happy and excited for a
man who's about to meet his death.

HEADMAN
Yes, captain, I'm chuffed to bits, I am. I ain't never
gonna 'ave to see that evil cow ever again! And I ain't
ever never not going to have to marry the evil cow! She
can't marry me if I'm dead, can she, Captain?

GREYLORD
I suppose not. Well I guess every cloud has a silver
lining.

*A whistle is blown and the troops position themselves to
charge, waiting for a final signal.*

WALKER
That ain't true, Captain. Not every cloud 'as a silver
lining. Some are, like, proper white and fluffy, and
others are all dark 'n' angry.

HEADMAN
He's got a point there, Captain. Not every cloud does
have a silver lining.

GREYLORD
And don't I know it, Private Headman.

HEADMAN
Well, I don't think you do, Captain, 'cos just a moment
ago you told me…

GREYLORD
What does it matter? It doesn't. Nothing does,
anymore, nothing.

WALKER
What about God?

HEADMAN
Blimey, you really are a prat. Hey, Captain Greylord,
didn't you hear me? I said he were a prat. Why aint y'
laughin', Captain? You're not laughing anymore.

GREYLORD
No, no, I'm not.

HEADMAN
Try 'n' look on the bright side of things.

WALKER
Yeah, it could always be worse.

GREYLORD
I'm about to be blown to smithereens. How could it
possibly be it any worse?

WALKER
Well, I dunno.

HEADMAN
He's got you there. Good one, Captain, you got him there! Ha ha...

The command is given to go over the top.